Mahadev

RENUKA NARAYANAN

PENGUIN
ANANDA

An imprint of Penguin Random House

PENGUIN ANANDA

USA | Canada | UK | Ireland | Australia
New Zealand | India | South Africa | China

Penguin Ananda is part of the Penguin Random House group of companies
whose addresses can be found at global.penguinrandomhouse.com

Published by Penguin Random House India Pvt. Ltd
7th Floor, Infinity Tower C, DLF Cyber City,
Gurgaon 122 002, Haryana, India

Penguin
Random House
India

First published in Penguin Ananda by Penguin Random House India 2019

10 9 8 7 6 5 4 3 2 1

ISBN 9780143447474

Typeset in Adobe Caslon Pro by Manipal Digital Systems, Manipal
Printed at Thomson Press India Ltd, New Delhi

www.penguin.co.in

MIX
Paper
FSC FSC® C010615

PENGUIN ANANDA

MAHADEV

Renuka Narayanan writes on religion and culture. She was the arts editor of the *Indian Express*, where she also wrote a column on religion for the editorial page. She was editor, Religion and Culture, *Hindustan Times* and the start-up director of the Indian Cultural Centre, Embassy of India, Bangkok.

Her published books include *The Book of Prayer*, *Faith: Filling the God-sized Hole*, *The Little Book of Indian Wisdom* and *The Path of Light: Tales from the Upanishads, Jatakas and Indic Folklore*.

She lives in Delhi.

Namas Parvati Pataye . . . Hara Hara Mahadeva!

1

Sadashiva Samarambham

'Who is Shiva?' asked the child.

'Nobody knows enough to really tell,' said her doting parents and grandparents. So they asked the family guru when he came by on a visit.

But he too shook his head. 'Nobody knew enough to really tell, even in the old days when the gods are said to have walked openly amidst us,' the guru said. '"*Tava tatvam na janami, kidrishosi, Maheshvara*, I do not know the true nature of your being, nor who you are, Great Lord". That's what it says in the *Shiva Mahimna Stotram*, an ancient Sanskrit hymn to Shiva, which many people recite even today. The great nineteenth-century saint Sri Ramakrishna Paramahamsa went into Samadhi, a deep yogic trance, while repeating it.'

'Tell me everything you know about Shiva!' said the child eagerly, and catching her mother's eye, hastily added, 'Please, Teacher.'

The guru looked gravely back at her. 'He remains a mystery despite the many stories about him,' he said.

'Even the Shiva Mahimnah Stotram, which lists many stories about Shiva, says that Shiva is too big a mystery for anyone to ever fully understand. Scholars say that this hymn may have been written by a person called Grahila, who poetically calls himself Pushpadanta, a gandharva or a heavenly musician, in the hymn. He famously says:

Asita-giri-samam syat kajjalam sindhu-patre
sura-taruvara-shak ha lekhani patra-murvi
likhati yadi grhitva sharada sarva-kalam
tadapi tava gunanam isha param na yati

O Lord, even if the black mountain was ink, the ocean the inkpot, a branch of the wish-fulfilling tree the pen, the earth the writing leaf, and if, taking these, the Goddess of Learning herself writes for all eternity, you cannot be completely described.

What a picture that paints! But we can say that we know two important things about Shiva. That he is one half of God. And that he dances.'

'Who is the other half of God?' said the child at once.

Her family smiled, knowing the delightful answer. Pleased that she had asked this question, they sat back and arranged themselves comfortably, the better to hear their guru say it.

'The other half of God is Shakti. We also call her Devi, Amba, Parvati, Gauri, Lalita, Kamakshi, Chandi, Chamundi; so many wonderful names, each with a story, just like Shiva,' said the guru, his face glowing with the lustre of saying the names aloud.

'So Shiva is half-woman?'

'Or Shakti is half-man. We can see it either way, or see them together as one, the way our people usually see them,' said the guru.

The child looked doubtfully at the teak-framed painting on the wall that showed Shiva and Parvati sitting side by side with their heavenly children Ganesha and Kartikeya on their laps. 'Then why do we see them like that?' she asked.

'God is actually the one Supersoul or the Paramatma. But it's hard to understand that properly. It does not satisfy our human need to pray to "Someone" who, we hope, understands us. We need a personality, an interesting one. So, logically, we try to understand the Creator through creation. What do we see? In our lush, tropical country we see that creation is full of natural forms *Aa Setu Himalaya*, meaning from the southernmost shore to the highest northenmost mountains or all the way from where the three oceans meet right up to the high Himalayas. This is our land, Bharatavarshe Jambudvipe. Bharatavarshe, the land of the Bharatas; Jambudvipe, the island of the rose-apple. So it seemed natural to us that the Creator revels in form. That's why we first saw and still see "God" in many ways—even as "gods" whom we think of as the expressions of the Supersoul.

'So an image like this, of the First Family, is really like a book. Each detail in it tells a story about the powers of God. We have many images to remind us of the many powers of God. And we have rules for iconography or spiritual art, called Murti Shilpa Shastra on how to make these images of God—as a god or goddess or divine family. We also have rules for iconometry, the system of measurement for making spiritual art, called Talamana. But it was Acharya who made us see the gods clearly in the first place,' said the guru.

'Who is Acharya?' asked the child.

'Acharya means a teacher. Here I mean Adi Shankara, the great teacher who went around India years and years ago risking life and limb to make religion clear to people,' said the guru.

'Jaya Jaya Shankara . . .' murmured the family in affirmation, hearing the beloved name.

The family guru nodded.

'Adi Shankara was named for Shiva, who is the Adi Guru or the first teacher,' he said. 'Adi means "the first" or "the beginning". To come close to understanding Shiva, we need to see him the way we originally saw him, through our own eyes, and not through the eyes of others. And one of the first and most important ways we see Shiva is as Dakshinamurthi, Lord of Learning. He sits on a raised rock under a banyan tree with one leg bent at the knee. This pose is called veerasana. Four sages, the Sanakadi yogis, are clustered at his feet like students. Lord Dakshinamurthi is Shiva as our first teacher, the Gurumurti.'

Meanwhile, the child's mother had Google-searched Dakshinamurthi's image on her phone and silently held it out.

The guru smiled. 'That's how he communicates, too, through silence. "Dakshina" means "gift" and also "south". And indeed, Dakshinamurthi looks southwards to gift us moksha or soul-liberation, since the south is the direction of moksha. Almost every old Indian temple, anywhere, has an image of Dakshinamurthi on its southern wall. Look for it the next time you visit a temple.'

'Of the twelve most ancient Shiva temples, the one at Ujjain has the shivling facing south. It's called "Mahakaleshwar", the Lord of Time. I was told it represents Dakshinamurthi,' volunteered the child's grandfather.

'I remember you took me there when I was about ten years old, really early in the morning,' said the child's father to his father, who was pleased that he remembered.

Meanwhile, the child and the guru pored over Dakshinamurthi's picture.

'See how young and peaceful his face is, with the crescent moon on his head. How the old sages look up to him. Among us, even a young guru, if knowledgeable, can have older disciples. Look how his eyes are closed in deep meditation and his body is pale, with sacred ash all over it,' said the guru. 'He's wearing a deerskin as a wrap and holding a japmala, a veena and a sanyasi's staff.'

'He has snakes around his wrists and ankles and neck. Why does he wear snakes?' said the insatiable child.

'I don't know the reason, either,' admitted the child's father.

'Oh, you've forgotten the lovely story about that,' said the child's grandmother. 'Naturally, everybody was afraid of snakes—people, birds, beasts—everybody! They didn't understand snakes at all. So they threw stones, snarled and shrieked at them. The snakes felt very bad about it. Wouldn't you, if nobody liked you and made it their business to hurt you? So they went wriggling in a body to

Shiva because they'd heard he was a strong, straightforward god with no fancy airs about him.'

'"Everybody hates us. We're so ashamed and depressed," they wept at his feet.'

'"Don't cry. You can live on my body if you like," said Shiva kindly.'

'The snakes cheered up at once. "Thank you, Great God! We never expected such a big honour!" they said, charmed by the perfection of the plan, for now everybody else would be so jealous. They began to fight good-naturedly about taking turns. The serpent Bhashaka won the honour of a permanent place on Shiva's very neck . . . around that beautiful blue throat.'

'I love that,' said the child's mother while the child flew to hug her grandmother, touched by Shiva's kindness to the weeping snakes but unable to express it in words.

'Didn't Bhashaka have a daughter called Ahilavati, who married Prince Ghatotkacha in the Mahabharata?' said the child's grandfather suddenly.

'You never told me that story!' exclaimed his son.

'I just remembered it,' smiled the grandfather. 'Your daughter's interest in Shiva is unlocking sealed, forgotten boxes in my head.'

'But why is Shiva's throat blue?' put in the child, and her parents exchanged a quick look, managing not to roll their eyes.

'I'll tell you next time. Or your grandparents or parents can,' smiled the guru, getting up.

'And miss hearing you say it? No, Guruji. Please come every Monday evening to tell us an instalment of the Shiv

Lila,' begged the elders. 'Let's keep it as a weekly tradition for the rest of the year, unless you're travelling, or we are.'

'It's so much nicer when you tell us the stories,' said the child's parents.

'Why on a Monday? What's "Shiv Lila"?' said the child, closely following the conversation.

'Each day of the week is special to some aspect of God. Monday is special to Mahadev, the Great God, as we love to call Shiva. We call God's stories a "lila", meaning "play or cosmic drama", because we choose to believe that everything is a game for God, whom we also call "the gods",' said the mother.

'Well said. Whenever we meet, let's share what we know about Shiva then!' suggested the guru.

'Shravanam, or listening to holy stories, will win us some merit as well,' enthused the grandmother.

Deep in their hearts, the Great God smiled. He liked it when people shared his stories. Doing that was supposed to make them calm, strong and affectionate. 'Just as they should be,' thought Shiva, and Parvati smiled, too, in amusement. There were going to be a few surprises. That was the very essence of Shiva. You never knew what he'd do next. Or what you might do, because of him.

2

Kalakuta

'You wanted to know why Shiva's throat is blue?' the guru asked the child on his next visit.

'Yes, please!' said the child.

'It's a strange, strong story, with beautiful ideas that we have never forgotten; ideas that people across Asia have shared and made their own, in many wonderful ways. Also, it tells you why we can't help loving Shiva,' said the guru slowly as though choosing his words with care.

'We're ready for it,' said the family as it settled happily on the carpet while the guru took a seat of honour facing them.

'A small greeting to God, first,' said the guru and everybody brought their palms together.

'Sri Ganeshaya Namaha,' said the guru first, 'honour to Lord Ganapati, with whose name we begin all things.' The family dropped their heads low over their hands.

'Namas Parvati-pataye,' said the guru, 'we bow to Parvati's husband.'

'Hara-Hara Mahadeva! Hail to the Great God!' said the family in one voice, even the child, for her mother had prepared her for this traditional sequence of call-and-response with which a teacher begins a session of telling holy stories.

'Janaki-kanta smaranam,' said the guru next, 'we remember Sita's beloved'.

'Jai-Jai Rama-Rama, victory to Rama,' responded the family.

'Sri Anjaneya murti ki . . .' came the guru's final call, 'to Lord Hanuman . . .'

'Jai,' rang the answer, 'everlasting triumph.'

The guru smiled at them and they smiled back, sealed in the ancient bond of teller and listener.

'You know how our ancestors saw the world,' began the guru. 'Brahma the Creator, hailed as Prajapati, the All-Father, created three main races: the celestials, the humans and the titans, called deva, manushya and asura in Sanskrit. They were each given one of the three realms of the universe—the celestial world called Svarg, the earth in the middle called Prithvi and the netherworld called Patal.'

'The celestials were light, airy beings, bathed in light. Their home, which they had named Indralok or Indra's World after their leader Indra or Sakra, was a fair realm through which they chased the lightning, played with the thunderclouds and rode the rain. They had everything they could possibly want. They were free from hunger, thirst, pain and perspiration. The flower garlands that they wore were ever fresh, and their feet did not touch the dusty ground. They had no need to work at or toil for anything, and they would never grow old and die. There was music and dance in their realm and golden goblets of a honeyed drink called mead, from "madhu", the Sanskrit word for "honey". They were the Immortals to whom the ones below had to offer sacrifice to obtain their favour and cooperation.'

'The earthlings were an interdependent race, much weaker than the celestials. Their home, the earth, was full of danger. They were exposed to the fury of the five elements and the rumblings and shakings of their terrain. Mountains rolled great boulders down on them, and mighty rivers broke their banks during the monsoon and washed the earthlings away with their dwellings of wattle and daub, thatch, wood and stone. Wolves and tigers tore them apart and tiny insects bit their skin, making them itch and scratch in pain. Sickness, old age and death claimed each one of them. No earthling—human, bird, beast, fish, reptile or insect—could escape that. The race of men had to think its way through every situation and work very hard to obtain the smallest ease or pleasure.'

'But though they were clearly interdependent, the race of men had proved greedy. They wanted to grab everything and hoard everything, be it cows, gold, land or the women of their species. They wanted more and more with every new thing. They fought and killed each other for the smallest reasons. Their greed was not merely for material goods. They revelled in saying and doing unkind things merely for the spiteful pleasure of hurting each other. But they also had the imagination to make new things that had never been seen before. And for all its perils and pitfalls, the earth they inhabited was so beautiful that even the celestials secretly coveted it.'

'The asuras or titans were a lumbering lot, gigantic in size, with strong, simple hearts. They loved their beautiful home, Patal, which glowed with treasures. Precious stones and minerals sparkled on the walls, silvery underground streams cooled the air and great iridescent serpents played with them and told them wonderful stories. However, the asuras revelled in their own strength and they hurt those weaker than themselves. They were marvellous beings capable of greatness, but their fatal flaw was their temper, which often made them cruel. Though theirs was an honourable race, too, created to keep the universe in balance, they were so jealous of the airy, confident celestials that they were always looking to score points over them and plotting attacks and invasions to take over the universe. Both the other races were wary of their violent ambition.'

'In this complicated situation, one fine morning, the king of devas, Indra, went by the ashram or hermitage of the sage Durvasa. Out of respect for Indra's position, the sage silently handed him a celestial santanaka flower that he happened to have by him. It was infused with the power of the vidyadharas, a race of magicians who could fly in the air and become invisible when they chose. But Indra had a vain moment and carelessly let the magic flower fall to the ground. The sage, who was already famous in all three worlds for his quick-trigger temper, let fly at Indra with a terrible curse.'

'"Wretched, mannerless creature!" stormed the sage, "you are unworthy of being a deva. I curse you twice over, once, to lose your riches, and secondly, I curse you and your race to fall ill, grow old and die like the earthlings!"'

'Indra hurriedly begged Durvasa's pardon and ran away but he was not really afraid. *Was he not an Immortal?* However, when the next asura attack on Svarg took place and some wounded devas actually died in battle, Indra was terrified. The devas managed to repel the asura attack that time but Indra knew the asuras would be back. He went straightaway to Brahma for a solution but, alas, the old Creator couldn't think of one.'

'"Let's ask Vishnu," said Brahma and they set out at once to Vaikunth, Vishnu's grand gem palace beyond the highest heaven where he lived in lonely splendour amidst golden pillars and gauzy clouds.'

'Bowing respectfully low, Indra told Vishnu his troubles and begged for help. They say that it was then that Vishnu, or Hari, as everyone loved to call him, meaning "destroyer of evil", first showed his godlike form, with four arms, his hands holding the disc, the conch, the mace and the most perfect lotus. His large, bright eyes were as lovely as lotus petals and his shapely hands and feet glowed as pink, while his heroic body blazed with divine light.'

'Indra and Brahma fell to their knees, stunned by his beauty and majesty. They looked hopefully at him.'

'"The time has come," said Vishnu, "to churn the Ocean of Milk at the edge of the universe. Many things were made and hidden there for safekeeping until their hour arrived. Nobody remembers or knows what its waves hide. But you devas cannot churn it on your own, the task is too big. Go speak softly to Bali, the king of the asuras, and his generals Ilvala and Pauloma, and make the asuras your partners. You must churn the Ocean of Milk together to dredge up amrita, the elixir of immortality that lies hidden in it. Take Mount Mandara as your churn, for it has the most likely shape and I will ask my great serpent Vasuki to be your churning rope.'"

"'Thank you, Lord. But I'm afraid the asuras are stronger than us, they will thrash us after the prize is won from the waves and leave us with nothing," said Indra anxiously.'

"'The asuras can't be allowed to turn into Immortals. The universe couldn't endure their ways," said Vishnu. "Don't worry. I'll be there, won't I?"'

'Indra looked sideways at Brahma and back at Vishnu.'

"'Don't mistake me, Lord," he said carefully, afraid of offending the almighty Preserver. "We know we will win, how can we not, with you on our side? But just in case something so terrible happens, that even you can't manage . . ."'

'A serene smile swept across Vishnu's face.'

"'Then there's always Shiva," he said.'

'As advised by Vishnu, Indra made his way cautiously to Patal and, in the custom of kings, was courteously received by King Bali, though with the hint of a swagger. Ignoring this provocation, Indra was all cordiality, and complimented Bali on the shimmering beauty of Patal's treasure-inlaid walls, its silver streams and scent-laden breeze. He humbly saluted Shukracharya, the learned and powerful asura guru, and conveyed greetings and gifts to him from Brihaspati, his own guru at the deva court. He presented King Bali an elephant-load of golden jars of mead. Then Indra diplomatically persuaded Bali to partner in the churning with artful hints about the treasures to be obtained. That hurdle cleared, he then cunningly set about securing an important advantage for the devas.'

'Knowing the contrary nature of the asuras and their deep jealousy of the devas, he airily declared that the devas would take the serpent's head side while churning. Ilavala and Pauloma, the asura generals, objected at once and soon the asura assembly was in angry uproar. So Indra pretended to give in unhappily and accept the "inferior" tail side, which delighted the asuras. Indra went away secretly laughing in satisfaction at having successfully negotiated which side of the great serpent his team would hold, just as he had intended all along!'

'On the appointed day, the two teams first uprooted the indignant Mount Mandara and bore it away, kicking and spewing boulders, to the Ocean of Milk where Vasuki waited. They looped the great serpent around Mandara, the asuras to Vasuki's head and the devas to Vasuki's tail and began to churn. But they had not wound Vasuki tightly enough and Mandara began to slip through Vasuki's loops. Vishnu had to hurriedly take the form of a kachhapa or giant turtle to provide a stable base on his back for Mandara in the wildly frothing ocean.'

The child's mother leaned forward at this point and held out her phone. She had found a picture of the enormous sculpture of this very scene that adorned the glittering airport of Suvarnabhumi, meaning 'golden land', at Bangkok. Everyone silently admired the brilliance of the powerful sculpture and the guru handed back the phone and resumed the story.

'How many wonderful things came out of the Ocean of Milk!'

'Ucchaisravas, the seven splendid steeds that galloped instinctively to Indra.'

'Airavat, the great white elephant, which meekly made its way, too, to Indra, and raised its trunk in salute.'

'Kamadhenu, Surabhi and Nandini, the bountiful wish-fulfilling cows, which ran mooing joyously to the devas and the watching sages as though to their natural protectors. The asuras barely noticed, heaving with all their might on the other side of Mandara.'

'The great bow Sharnga appeared and went to Vishnu, which is why he came to be called "Sharngapani", holder of the Sharnga. It's "Sharnga", by the way, not "Saranga", which means "dappled", like a deer.'

'Some say that the beautiful dancers, the apsaras, came up from the ocean, too, but the Srimad Bhagavatam, which is Sri Krishna's life story, says they were the daughters of a sage.'

'Three rare gems came floating up—the ruby-red Kaustubh, which went of its own accord to Vishnu to live on his chest; the glittering white Chintamani with sparks of fire in it, a wish-fulfiller that Indra hastily tucked into his waistband, securing his wealth for good; and the elegant; and pale yellow Chudamani, which was to have its own poignant adventures.'

'A flowering tree emerged, filling the air with sweetness and refreshing the exhausted devas and asuras. It floated over the devas, shedding its milk white- and-coral blossoms on them before heading to the Gandhamadana gardens in Indralok.'

'A shining, handsome young figure rose up next, holding a golden pot. It was the divine healer, Dhanvantari, carrying the amrita or sudha, the elixir of immortality. A roar of triumph greeted him, but, receiving a silent command from Vishnu, he stood aside on the beach and signalled to the panting devas and asuras to keep churning.'

'The moon rose up then and soared up into the sky where it palely hovered, clearly having decided to wait its turn.'

'And finally, the greatest treasure of all, Lakshmi, floated up from the ocean, causing a stunned silence to fall on all creation, which had never seen a lovelier vision. The skies rained flowers on her and Varuna, lord of the waters, rose up himself to hand her the vyjayantimala, the rarest of rare garlands, made of precious gems and flowers.'

'Lakshmi looked around her cautiously and saw the resplendent black form and beautiful face of Vishnu. In that awed cosmic silence, she went straight to Vishnu, put the garland around his neck and nestled on his broad chest next to the Kaustubh.'

'A deep sigh went up from all around at the perfection of that sight, at the utter beauty of the divine couple. No more was Hari alone, he now had Sri, good fortune incarnate by his side, to bless earth with!'

'They turned now to the business of distributing the amrita and such a quarrel broke out that desperate measures were called for. Vishnu, who had already taken the form of the kachhapa, tortoise and had also stood by directing proceedings in his godlike, four-armed form, now rushed to take yet another form as Mohini, the enchantress; and took up the pot of amrita, cleverly giving the devas almost every drop of it.'

'The asuras went back fuming, to Patal while the devas cheered and cheered their commander and saviour, Vishnu.'

'But Vishnu flung up a hand for silence.'

'"Let us thank the one who saved us all," he said and meditated on Shiva, who appeared, smiling calmly, with Parvati by his side.'

'"Mahadev, if you had not done what you did . . ." said Vishnu gravely.'

'The devas shuddered, thinking of it . . .'

'When the churning had settled into a rhythm after Vishnu provided a stable base for Mandara, Vasuki had been squeezed so unbearably that he began to belch great gusts of poisonous breath. The asuras, whom Indra had tricked into holding the head side, suffered hideous agonies from the fumes. Vishnu had had to summon up a strong breeze to clear the air and cleanse the sky.'

'But Nature had its own inscrutable laws by which every action had consequences and the churning had required them to take a great risk with nature. There came another, even deadlier danger that no one had anticipated.'

'What had happened was that Vasuki's poison had stirred up an even greater poison, the Kalakuta or Halahala, out of the depths of the ocean. It rose up in a foul gust, darkening the sky and threatening to destroy every living creature in all three worlds.'

'Nobody knew what to do about it, it was so immense and overpowering, a gigantic cloud of death that shot up into the sky from the ocean bed and threatened to invade every pore of the three worlds.'

'While the universe wilted helplessly, Vishnu had prayed to Shiva to come and save the situation. Without an instant's delay, Shiva had appeared, waded into the ocean, cupped his hands and—drunk up the poison! There was nowhere in the universe to send the Kalakuta, aptly named "the bane of death itself". Only the Great God could hope to tackle it and save the world. He had done so at once without a thought for himself.'

'So strong was the Kalakuta that it had begun to burn even Shiva from within. But Parvati, who had followed him to the ocean, had stopped the poison with the power of her divine earrings, the tatankam, which bore the force of the sri chakra yantra, a power diagram. She had touched her earrings for an extra boost of energy and put her delicate hand on Shiva's neck. The poison had halted with its fire spent, and pooled in his pale throat, turning it dark blue. Shiva was often to be hailed after that as "Nilkanth", the one with the blue throat. But having done this unimaginably selfless deed, he had quietly gone back to his home on Mount Kailash . . .'

'As Shiva stood with Parvati on the shore of the ocean, Vishnu looked up at the moon, which patiently awaited direction after floating up into the sky as a graceful crescent.'

'"How cool and mild this son of the sea looks," thought Vishnu. "It should go to Shiva for having swallowed that world-destroying poison without a word of protest or complaint, and quietly retreating after that, not wanting a thing for himself. How could anyone be so selfless? Chandra, the Moon, must go to him."'

'Vishnu nodded at the lovely crescent, which then sailed across to Shiva's head and attached itself elegantly to his topknot of wild, matted hair. Shiva smiled and patted it in welcome.'

'"Thank you," he said charmingly to Vishnu.'

'But Vishnu was not done yet. He presented the precious gem Chudamani to Shiva to wear as a shikhamani or crest-jewel. Shiva thanked Vishnu affectionately but since he did not really wear jewellery like others did, he handed it to Parvati, who clipped it gaily in her hair . . .'

'But, Guruji,' said the grandmother, after the guru paused to let his listeners enjoy the elation and wonder of the moment, 'I never knew that the Chudamani had a connection with Shiva. I thought it was Sita's.'

'You're right, and it became Sita's in an interesting way. Once, when Parvati flew over the great curve of the earth, a high breeze blew her hair about. The Chudamani that she wore as a sort of hairclip was loosened and fell to earth. Parvati looked down to see where it had fallen. She saw that it had landed in the garden of the Janaka Seeradhvaj in Videha and a little girl had picked it up and was playing with it. That little girl was Sita Vaidehi, and that's how she got the Chudamani. Parvati laughed when she saw who it was and flew on, thinking, "Let her keep it." But that's Parvati for you.'

'Didn't Shiva mind?' said the child's mother, smiling.

'Not in the least,' laughed the guru. 'He would wear only rudraksha beads, if at all. He has no interest in finery. And we know it. While we love to dress up the idols of every other god and goddess as kings, queens and royal babies, we don't dare festoon Shiva with frills. Instead, we tiptoe carefully around him. In fact, we say *"abhishekha priyo Shiva, alankara priyo Vishnu"*. This means that Shiva loves being offered just water and bel leaves, if we can get them, while Vishnu enjoys decoration, even if it's just a small sprig of aromatic tulsi leaves. So we, as devotees, can keep our offerings to our gods as simple or grand as we want. It's our love that they value. That's why it was not out of character for Parvati to let Sita keep the precious Chudamani.'

'Wasn't Sita's father's name just "Janaka"?' asked the child's father.

'Janaka was the name for a very wise and spiritually evolved ruler. Sita's father Seeradhvaj was one such king, which is why he was called Janaka, it was actually a title,' said the guru.

'I've always wondered how Rama managed to keep his ring and Sita her jewellery in exile. I thought Kaikeyi personally supervised the removal of their royal finery before they left Ayodhya for the forest,' said the child's mother.

'That's a good point,' said the guru. 'That was because nobody could touch the jewellery that Sita brought from her father's home, including the Chudamani that she would one day give Hanuman to give Rama, when Hanuman found her in Lanka. And Kaikeyi could not take away Rama's ring either, the one he would give Hanuman to give Sita, because it was Janaka's gift to him; a present from Videha, not Ayodhya.'

'How the details interest us even after millennia,' marvelled the grandmother.

'These stories are in our very bones,' laughed the young father, patting his wide-eyed child's head.

'There's the strangest afterword, linking the Kalakuta to the Mahabharata as well,' said the guru. 'As you know, when Shiva drank up the deadly poison, it began to burn his throat. The vish purush or spirit of Kalakuta sprang out of Shiva weeping in shame at the outrage he had involuntarily committed by burning Shiva's throat and in despair at the ferocity of his substance. So the Lord, who wanted nothing for himself but gave things away to others, blessed him with a boon, for it was not Kalakuta's fault that it was so deadly. It had lain quietly at the bottom of the ocean, not getting in anybody's way. It grew fierce only when fiddled with, and brought out just as so many other things are poisonous if we stir them up ourselves. So it couldn't help being part of Nature's chemical laws and neither could the vish purush as Kalakuta's inner spirit person.'

'Lord Shiva granted the vish purush the boon that he would return to Nature by being born on earth one day as the son of Drona and would kill his father's enemies. So the vish purush was born as Ashvatthama; and Vishnu himself, as Sri Krishna, had to fend him off. Ashvatthama's spirit is said to still wander the earth, quietly and is called out only if and when we stir up terrible world-destroying poisons . . . like nuclear bombs, I should think.'

'That's horrible!' cried the mother.

'I feel bad for Ashvatthama,' said the father.

'It's a waste of pity, if you don't mind my saying so,' said the guru. 'He wasted his human birth. He was very proud and vain, and at the same time, very much the fawning courtier to wicked Duryodhana. If Vyasa did not pity Ashvatthama, we need not either.'

'I find that a remarkably matter-of-fact attitude, accepting both "good" and "bad" as just things that are,' mused the grandfather.

'And that there are always consequences when something is done,' said the grandmother.

'So now you know why Shiva's throat is blue,' said the guru to the child. 'What do you think of it all?'

'I think our gods do a lot for us,' said the child seriously.

3

Vipareet

'I've been haunted all week by the thought that Ashvatthama is still roaming about,' said the child's mother when the guru came by next. 'Is there anything else on earth from when the gods are said to have walked openly amidst us?'

'The whole universe is witness to the sport of the gods,' said the guru mock-pompously, to make her laugh. 'But where is the child?'

'There's an extra music lesson today, instead of tomorrow. She has a friend in class whose mother will drop her home soon, we take turns,' said the mother.

'Meanwhile, please won't you tell us about witnesses on earth to epic times?' said the grandmother. 'I'm longing to know, too.'

'Of course, I will. I'm so glad to have such a question to try answering,' said the guru.

'In the epics themselves, the seven most important witnesses to Vishnu, whom he personally saved, are Prahlad, Vibhishana, Gajendra, Draupadi, Ahalya,

Arjuna and Dhruva. And on earth, there are four things in Mathura-Vrindavan that are celebrated as being from "before Sri Krishna's time", meaning he actually touched them in the epics: the river Yamuna, Mount Goverdhan, "Brajraj", the soil of the Brajbhumi region, and the temple to Parvati as Devi Katyayani.'

'That's a lovely swathe of sacred geography,' said the mother. 'What about Shiva? Are there such landmarks for him?'

'Besides Mount Kailash, you mean?' said the grandfather.

'Yes, indeed. Besides Mount Kailash, there are many important epic witnesses on earth to Shiva. Top of the mind are the rivers Ganga and Yamuna, the twelve Jyotirlingas or ancient Shiva temples which make a grid across India, and Chidambaram, the only place on earth said to have witnessed his dance of joy, the Ananda Tandava. Shiva has been worshipped at Chidambaram for over two thousand years as "Koothan", the Dancer, and as "Nataraja", the Lord of Dance,' said the guru.

'I want us all to go there one day,' said the grandfather. 'I want us to experience these places together. It would be wonderful to see at least a few. Please come with us if that happens, Guruji, to make it complete for us.'

'I certainly shall, if possible. But today, I feel I must tell you about the first of two most endearing and wise witness to Shiva. This god is also the most accessible deity that anyone ever had. Your questions have made him shine in my mind. No guessing, please, grownups! Let's give the child a chance to guess when she gets home,' laughed the guru.

'I can't resist asking just the one thing. Is he the god about whom some scholars made those Freudian interpretations that were in fashion decades ago in Western scholarship?' asked the grandfather.

'Meaning that there was jealousy about his mother between him and his father?' said the grandmother, making a face. 'One knows that there are many dark shades to many human relationships. But why would they want to try and force our gods through that filter?'

'It was a passing phase out West that's dated now. Meanwhile, the gods shine on for us undimmed,' said the guru.

'Good we got that out of the way without the child around,' said the grandmother as the front door bell rang and the mother got up.

'The old stories are so complex and coded that often, there's a huge gap between our lived reality of faith and what a commentator says from outside about our intense inner world. It does not touch us,' said the child's father. 'I read many critical things, too, but they seem like shadows and they lead me nowhere. In fact, I come back with my allegiance to the gods renewed.'

'Well, that's what most of us seem to have done down the centuries in the face of hostility, we've only grown even more attached to the gods. It's a staunch and stubborn love. I think it's worth having. The Jews have a similar love. The Old Testament says that when the Red Sea parted to let the slave Jews escape the Pharaoh of Egypt, one young woman actually took her lyre with her. She was so sure god would take her safely across.

What does that say about having total faith? It's deeply moving.

'Think of how Vasudeva set his trembling feet with total faith in the roaring waters of the Yamuna when she parted during that torrential downpour to let him cross with his precious burden. Our abiding love is what we should keep in mind as the larger picture or deeper reality. People, with or without scholarship, have always said things. But our religion itself exists because somebody or the other within it kept asking questions,' said the guru.

'Our religion is unique in several ways. One such point is that we do not have just one holy book. We have a library. Two, doubts and questions were allowed right from the earliest text, the Rig Veda. The Upanishads are full of people who asked questions—Nachiketas, Janaka, Gargi, Bhrigu—and they all got answers. Yajnavalkya's answer to Janaka and Gargi are absolutely epic. We find them in the Brihadaranyaka Upanishad.'

'Valmiki asked Narada about a perfect man and we got the Srimad Ramayanam. Draupadi asked questions about the law in the Kaurava court that ring in our ears even today. Arjuna asked Krishna questions and we got the Bhagavad Gita. Dhritarashtra asked Sanjay what was going on in Kurukshetra and we got the story of the battle. He also asked questions of Vidura and got the Sanat Sujatiyam. The yaksha by the pond asked Yudhishtira questions and we got the famous Yaksha Prashna. Yudhishtira asked Bhishma on his bed of arrows about God and got the Vishnu Sahasra Namam. He asked questions about good governance, too, and was duly answered. Vyasa asked Narada why he felt depressed after composing the Mahabharata and because of Narada's reply that Vyasa had not written much about Krishna in the Mahabharata, Vyasa set to work again and composed the Srimad Bhagavatam.'

'Vyasa taught it only to his son Shuka. But when King Parikshit, who had but a week to live, asked Shuka Brahmam for the story, we got the Srimad Bhagavatam, too. The Bhagavatam is called "the ripe fruit of the Vedas made available by Shuka for all to relish its nectar":

nigama-kalpa-taror galitaṁ phalaṁ
śuka-mukhād amṛta-drava-saṁyutam
pibata bhāgavataṁ rasam ālayaṁ
muhur aho rasikā bhuvi bhāvukāḥ'

'Can you imagine not knowing about Dhruva, Prahlad and Gajendra? Can you imagine not knowing about Rama and Krishna? Speaking for myself, life would be a howling wilderness for me without them. So I think our holiest and truest symbol, more than even the swastika or Om, is the prashneeyam—the question mark.'

'Questions come from intentions, don't they?' said the grandfather.

'I take your point. The intention matters. You can see it in the tone of the writing and in the way the content is presented. Our religion certainly teaches us not to flinch from the truth. That gives us an open door to reform. However, a critique of the gods, though scholarly or well-written, does not automatically become "truth". So there's that side as well to being "open minded",' said the guru.

'A good case in point is the nineteenth-century epic poem Meghnad Badh Kavya by Michael Madhusudan Dutt. It has nine cantos. My Bengali friends assure me that it's a brilliant poem. But in it, Dutt valorizes Ravana's son Meghnath, also known as Indrajit, and negatively portrays Rama and Lakshmana.'

'Why did Dutt do that? The fact is that our religion was not doing well in the nineteenth century. Many terrible social practices had taken root over time and ghastly superstitions harmed the people. We mustn't defend the indefensible but look to reform. The horror is still not entirely over, alas. It continues to haunt our society despite the sincere efforts of so many to change for the better. But change it will. It's an irreversible process.'

'Dutt was clearly a learned, sensitive person. He had an English education in Calcutta and rebelled against stagnant old ways. But he did not take to fighting. This was done by so many bold, sincere Hindu reformers across society.'

'Not just the great and famous reformers like Ram Mohun Roy, Ishwar Chandra Vidyasagar and Rabindranath Tagore but thousands of ordinary, unknown, unsung Hindus in family after family who made brave personal choices to set an example, to fight their own orthodoxy, to stand up courageously against the wrath of their own elders and the paralysing fear of "what will people say" and "who will marry your sisters". They did that from within society, often at great personal cost.'

'If it were not for all those people before us who valiantly tried to change our society with true Shiva tattva in their heart, we would not be sitting together so comfortably today or have whatever freedoms we now have. So it would be churlish and ungrateful to kick the ladder we climbed.'

'But this was not a choice that Dutt made. Instead, he took what may look like a shortcut or an escape route to us, though to him it may have seemed the only available path to personal modernity those days. He became a Christian, left Calcutta to move to Madras, married an Indo-Briton out there and wrote furiously.'

'In his new identity, he spurned Rama as a foundational figure of our faith although it was not the God's fault but man's that our society had grown unbearable in the way it treated its own people. So yes, the author's intention, or "where he's coming from" is a factor. But one cannot dislike Dutt for it given that our ways had become so cruel and stifling.'

'Dutt wrote reams in English and wanted to live in England. He desperately wanted to be English. He sent poem after poem in English to literary magazines in England but they refused to publish them and he had to publish his own work in Madras. Finally, it was in his mother tongue, Bengali, and by writing about the Ramayana, that he became famous. Interesting, is it not? Epic grace obviously touched him.'

'The Rama we look up to is found in the *mool* or root epic, Srimad Ramayanam by Valmiki. In fact, even the scope for later poets to portray Meghnath or Ravana according to their creative fancy is found right there in the Srimad Ramayanam itself, for it is so full of texture and shades. It's not a flat, "goody-goody" story at all. That is

Valmiki's genius. That is the Rama whom we cannot bear to be parted from, of whom Tulsidas said in the sixteenth century, "Janani, main na jiyoon bin Ram (Mother, I cannot live without Ram)". Why do you think Rama has outlasted all critics in the hearts of millions of ordinary people although he's had so much criticism since the nineteenth century? That's because at the end of the debate, if debate we must, we have the emotional right to Rama just as we have the right to Shiva and Shakti. And we keep that right despite everything that's gone on—or goes on now.'

'It's not an easy place for us,' said the grandfather grimly as the child came in after changing out of her school clothes and drinking a glass of milk. Her mother brought in a tray with small bowls of cut fruit and the child's father got up to take the tray from her.

After tea, biscuits and fruit, the family settled down to hear the day's story.

'What will you tell us about Shiva today, Teacher?' said the child, innocently unaware of the darkness that always marched with light.

4

Gajanan

'Can you guess who our cuddliest god is?' said the guru to the child.

'Baby Krishna,' said the child at once.

'Wonderful!' exclaimed the grandfather as everybody laughed in appreciation.

The guru smiled broadly. 'You're right,' he told the child, and to the grown-ups, he said, 'sometimes we have to learn from our children, like Shiva learnt an important thing from his younger son, Kumar.'

'Let me put it differently,' he smiled at the child. 'Who is Shiva's eldest son?'

'Ganapati,' said the child promptly.

'Can you describe him?'

The child looked at her mother, who nodded.

The child put her hands together in namaste and recited:

'Mushika vahana modaka hasta
Chamara karna vilambita sutra

Vamana rupa Maheshvara putra
Vighna Vinayaka pada Namaste'

'Very good,' murmured the guru. 'Do you know the meaning as well?'

'Would you like to show it in dance with your hands while I recite it for you?' said the mother gently, to encourage the child to express herself.

The child's eyes lit up even as she nodded a little shyly, and she stood on the carpet to demonstrate the prayer through the mudras she had recently learnt in dance class.

They applauded when she finished with a namaste.

'Now who will translate it into words?' said the guru.

'Let me try,' said the child's father and shut his eyes for a moment to invoke Ganapati's blessings, before he said:

'Whose vehicle is the mouse and who holds a sweet in his hand,

Whose large ears are like fans and who wears a long sacred thread,

Who is compact in stature and is the son of Maheswara, Lord Shiva

I bow at the feet of that "Vighna Vinayaka", the Remover of the Obstacles for us, his devotees.'

'A good attempt and absolutely correct,' said the guru. 'That's not an easy thing to do at all because Indian poetry, especially from Sanskrit, is very difficult to translate satisfactorily into English. It's almost impossible to get the rhythm even though you get close to the meaning. But I see that you are all like Ganapati in wanting to know the meaning of things. Your daughter has got this good habit of questioning and finding out from you all.'

'We've taught her to do what our parents did for us,' smiled the mother. 'For instance, each time I came across a new word, my father trained me to look it up at once in the Shabda Kosh or the Dictionary. Today we just ask "Googleshvar", it's all become so easy with technology!'

'Does Ganapati also like to learn things?' asked the child.

'Oh, yes! He's very particular about understanding something properly. That's why we like to see him with an elephant head since we consider the elephant the noblest and wisest of beasts,' said the guru.

'I heard a story in school that his father cut his real head off and replaced it with an elephant's head,' said the child questioningly.

'The old myths are strange and strong, like I said when I told you the tale of Kalakuta. They are from so long ago that there are several versions of them. It's as though people down thousands of years couldn't resist retelling them, sometimes with extra spice. One version goes that Shiva asked for proof of his son's love and Ganapati instantly offered his own head, which was then replaced with an elephant's head. Sacrifice is a big theme in old religious stories, you know, like how Yahweh, the tribal god of the Jews, asked Abraham to sacrifice his son Izak as a proof of love.'

'Then, for instance, there's the story that Ganapati broke off a tusk to take dictation; to use it as a stylus on palm leaves to write down the story of the Mahabharata as Vyasa composed it and said it aloud. But another, even more powerful story goes that Ganapati just let his tusk be broken by the angry sage Parshurama, out of respect for his father, since Parshurama had thrown an axe at him that belonged to Shiva. Imagine that level of respect,' said the guru.

'I don't know that story at all, do tell us,' entreated the mother.

'I certainly shall. But before that, I would like to clear the ground in general about having different versions to a story. Since Rama was an ardent devotee of Shiva, who was his aradhya or beloved personal deity, let's take the Ramayana. It is said to have over three hundred and twenty five versions in India alone. There are more versions all over Asia. The Ramayana is "the Epic of Asia" in ways not fully counted yet. There's even a version in Mongolia in the far north and in Japan in the farthest east.'

'I, as a believer, like the root Ramayana best, which is Valmiki's. Also, I stay with Valmiki's first six books, which end with the hero's homecoming, coronation, and the phala shruti or list of listener's benefits. So the Ramayana ends for me with its sixth book, the Yuddha Kandam,' said the guru.

'What makes you do that, Teacher?' said the grandfather, startled.

'I choose to stick with the root story because I don't want to be confused, or confuse others. There's a seventh book to Valmiki's Ramayana, the Uttara Kandam, which has dubious twists like the killing of a non-kshatriya, Shambuka, and Rama sending pregnant Sita away to the forest, their twin sons, and their terrible last parting. It doesn't fit Rama's character as built up in the first six chapters that end with the phala shruti, which always comes at the end. So the seventh chapter seems tacked on later. It does not seem in keeping with Valmiki in some scholarly opinion, which suits me.'

'Valmiki began the Ramayana by asking Sage Narada, "*Kon asmin sampratam loke gunavan?* (Which man, in this present world, is the man with the ideal qualities?)" He then lists sixteen ideal qualities, which include dharmagnyascha— of righteous conduct. It was a contemporary account, an itihasa, meaning "as it happened". Sending Sita away like that simply does not fit. So I find it impossible to accept the Uttara Kandam, although it's so well-known.'

'But then, Valmiki didn't have Ahalya turn to stone either. Her husband Rishi Gautama merely curses her to become invisible and immovable at home in their ashram until liberated by Rama. He says, "You will remain here unseen, lying on the ashes, with the air as your food. One day, Rama, the son of Dasaratha, will enter this ashram. His presence will make our home blessed again and restore you".'

'Rama never put his foot on her. Can you imagine him doing that to a woman? As he went by, it was the dust from the paduka on his feet that flew up and landed on Ahalya where she lay unseen, which brought her back. After setting Ahalya free, when Rama, Lakshmana and Vishvamitra arrive in Mithila, Vishvamitra tells Sita's father of their adventures. Janaka's high priest, Sadananda the Rajguru, sheds tears of joy to hear this account for he is Ahalya's son and overcome with emotion that his mother is back and his parents are together again. So it wasn't Valmiki at all, but Kalidasa who turned Ahalya into stone in his *Raghuvamsha*—and others after him did so, too. Valmiki didn't have a "Lakshman rekha" either. Did you know that it was Tulsidas's invention?'

'Incredible!' said the father, 'These notions have taken such deep root in the public mind.'

'Well, I, for one, curl my lip at the "Lakshman rekha" as a literal device that's medievally prudish and I feel sure that Valmiki would curl his lip, too,' said the guru, making a rueful face.

'In the root Ramayana, Ravana drags Sita away by her hair and holds her in his arms. But Tulsi, gallant soul, obviously couldn't handle the thought in the sixteenth century of Ravana laying hands on Sita and neither could others elsewhere, so they respectfully or prudishly changed it. Therefore, it's about them, not the epic. Much as I honour and appreciate Tulsi's concern, it's another reason why I choose to clinically stick to the original Valmiki.'

'It's the Ramayana "as it is" without the little zari curtains and pyjamas,' smiled the grandmother.

'Exactly!' said the guru. 'But Tulsi had great clarity on the larger picture. He rescued religion with his "people's Ramayana", the *Ramcharitmanas*, composed in Avadhi, the everyday dialect of his region. It simplified matters for the common man. Tulsidas, as noted by Ramayana scholars, observed that the public was prone to be easily impressed and misled by all kinds of fantastical ascetics and their doctrines.'

'Tulsi disapproved of yogis who grew long nails, bound their hair in dreadlocks, wore strange, frightening ornaments and, so to speak, dressed for the fairground. He said in another work, the *Vinay Patrika*, that "*Bahumat muni bahu panth puranani, jahan-tahan jhagaro*", meaning that seers profess many opinions, there are many old stories about many paths to salvation, and there are quarrels all over the place.'

'He said that real religion was much less complicated, that it was a direct connection between a soul and God, whom he was personally taught by his guru to see as Rama.'

'Therefore, Tulsidas's repeated spiritual advisory for people living out their lives in this particular age, which we called Kalyug, was brief and straightforward: "*Kalyug jog na jagya na gnana / Ek aadhar Ram gun gaana* (In Kalyug, neither austerity, nor sacrifice nor deep knowledge is required / Singing in praise of Ram is the only path to salvation)".'

'The public of the day could not resist the triple impact of the simplicity of Tulsi's case, the heartbreaking appeal of Valmiki's story that Tulsi retold with his own twists like the "Lakshman rekha" incident, and Tulsi's poetry, which seemed simple but was in fact profoundly musical and meaningful. So the history of religion in North India changed forever with the *Ramcharitmanas*.'

'Awesome,' said the father wonderingly while the fascinated elders nodded in recognition of the truth in their guru's words.

'But I don't understand how anyone could write that a very proper person like Rama banished his pregnant wife to the forest. It's unbearable!' said the mother.

'It's a terrible mystery that's never stopped tormenting us. If you indeed accept the seventh book, the Uttara Kandam, as Valmiki's—which, by the way, no traditional religious speaker discourses on—your only acceptable explanation is that given by the Right Honourable V.S. Srinivasa Sastri.'

'Shastri was born to very poor rural priest and came up by his own hard work. He became a silver-tongued Independence activist, administrator and educator. He was born the same year as Gandhi, in 1869, and died in 1946. He was totally against the idea of Partition. I have a copy of his book, *Lectures on the Ramayana*. It contains the thirty public lectures that he gave in 1944 in Madras. He boldly pointed out that "to err is human" and since Rama was in human avatar, he made "a great mistake" putting his royal duty as he saw it above justice to his innocent wife.'

'There is only one small consolation to be found here, and even that takes a bit of detective work. You can find it in the discourses by young, modern religious speakers. Such a speaker would point out first of all that Valmiki's ashram in the woods was one of the places visited by Rama, Sita and Lakshmana during their exile, so he was known to them.'

'Valmiki, whose original name was Harit, had meditated for so long that an "anthill", a termite mound, really, called "vaalmeek" in Sanskrit, grew to enclose him. So when Harit emerged one day from the mound, he was called "Valmiki", "of the mound". It was a like a new birth for him. The Vedas say that such termite mounds are "the ears of Mother Earth". So since Valmiki was "reborn" from the "ear" of Mother Earth, he was figuratively her son. That is the next point.'

'Now we know that Sita, too, was found on the ground by Janaka, she was a daughter of Mother Earth, which is why she has names like Bhumija, Kshitija and Avanija, all meaning "Earth's Daughter". It's the custom, even today, for a woman to go to her mother's house, or brother's, to have her babies. Since Valmiki and Sita were both children of Mother Earth, they were technically siblings. So Rama ordered Lakshman to leave Sita near Valmiki's hermitage and Valmiki took her home, exactly as set up. Valmiki was about sixty-two then and Sita, thirty-five. He was a very fatherly brother to her.'

'We have to cull these points and join the dots to console ourselves that Rama, a very correctly behaved person, was being proper in this as well. He didn't abandon her just anywhere out in the wild, nor did Valmiki find her just by chance, as popular TV serials may depict. She was sent where he would find her.'

'There's something there, I suppose,' said the mother, wiping away her tears for Sita.

'It's almost too ironic. "Videha" means "bodiless". Yet Sita Vaidehi was judged physically for being kidnapped,' said the guru.

'But what about Ganapati's tusk?' said the child, not wanting to lose her story in this grown-up talk.

'I'm about to tell you,' smiled the guru.

'The story goes that Sage Vyasa wanted to dictate an epic poem, the Mahabharata. He needed someone to write it down as it flowed from his mind. Nobody capable was found to exist on earth, so he approached Ganapati or Ganesha, meaning "leader of Shiva's troops, the ganas". Ganapati was also known as Gajanan, meaning "elephant head" and Vighna Vinayaka, the remover of obstacles. Vyasa requested him to help out.'

'Take dictation?' said Ganapati.

'If you please,' said Vyasa.

'Very well, I shall,' said Ganapati, but added the condition, 'You must not stop at any point or I shall stop writing and go away.'

'We're taught that the gods love to twist the odds for men just to see how we will react, since Creation is their divine play or lila. Since Vyasa was clever—he had to be, to compose a long and complicated epic like the Mahabharata—he made a counter-condition that Ganapati had to understand every word before he wrote it down. Ganapati was pleased to agree, secretly delighted by this clever move of Vyasa's. He broke off his own tusk to write with, as proof of goodwill, and they began the task.'

'Every now and then, Vyasa would compose a number of verses in extremely layered and dense language. Ganapati would have to pause to think them through before putting them down on the palm-leaf pages. This allowed Vyasa to draw breath and compose more verses in his head, to stay ahead.'

'We had a workshop at office in which this story came up,' said the father to the guru. 'Vyasa's response to Ganapati's proviso was pointed out as an example of an organic solution to a problem. Vyasa came up with this pragmatic strategy because he was goal-oriented and intent on fulfilling his mission. They said that this legend was a popular teaching story to inspire focus and concentration, and that its iconic reminder in daily life is the broken tusk on all Ganapati idols.'

'An excellent point,' said the guru.

'What's the second story about Ganesha's tusk, please, Teacher?' said the child.

'Years ago I saw this story beautifully danced in Thailand in their classical dance style called Khon, and I still relish the memory. The story is from the Brahmanda Purana. It tells of Parshurama or Rama of the Axe who was Lord Vishnu's sixth avatar. He is believed to have never really gone away but to be meditating even now on earth in a secret cave in the mountains.'

'Lord Shiva had given Parshurama the axe to help him fight the tyrant Kartavirya. When Parshurama's task was over, he made his way to Mount Kailash where Shiva lived, to return the axe and thank him. But at the mystic mountain, he found his path blocked by Ganapati. Lord Shiva had ordered his son to guard Mount Kailash against all visitors since he was about to go into a long, deep trance and did not want to be disturbed.'

'Parshurama, a devotee of Shiva, was furious at being blocked by Ganapati. "Ho, Devaputr! Move away!" he raged. But Ganapati stood calm and immovable. Losing his temper, Parshurama forgot all propriety and hurled the axe at the Devaputr, the Son of God.'

'Ganapati could have easily deflected the axe. But since it belonged to his father, he did not stop it out of love and respect and let it break his tusk. He couldn't help crying out in pain though at the force of the blow. Parvati appeared at once, hearing his cry, and roundly ticked off Parshurama for hurting her child. But Shiva was very proud of his staunch, loving son and Ganapati proudly carries his broken tusk ever after because of that.'

'So which story is the right one here—and about the elephant head?' asked the child.

'You may choose, like I have with the Ramayana,' said the guru, in all seriousness.

The family held its breath while the child thought it over.

'Ganapati loved his father very much, didn't he? So I choose the story about him offering his head himself. That fits with the tusk story that Ganapati let Parshurama break it because he loved his father,' said the child.

The family looked quietly at one another, waiting for the guru's reaction.

The guru smiled. 'A good choice,' he said affectionately. '*Shiva prema pindam bhaje vakra tundam* (Hail the Lord with the broken tusk who is Shiva's own darling).' And privately, he thought, 'Sound emotional logic. How much one learns from children!' which was the silent opinion of the child's family as well.

'So Parshurama, like Ashvatthama, never went away from earth,' noted the mother.

'It's intriguing how these ancient stories animated so many minds across space and time, and continue to do so,' said the grandfather.

'And how people still make modaka for Ganapati's birthday,' said the grandmother. 'I can't imagine why I stopped making them when you went away to college,' she told her son, who threw up his hands, smiling.

'I wonder if you would like to make a royal umbrella for Ganapati this year on his birthday,' she said to the child.

'I would! How do I do it?'

'This is a sweet custom for children. When I was a little girl, we had neighbours from many places in India and we happily shared each other's food and some special customs. So, a month before Ganapati's birthday, which we call "Ganesh Chaturthi", I, like the other children in my little group of boys and girls, was told to save and smooth out toffee wrappers in jewel colours for Ganapati's umbrella for our pujas at home. My mother and I would then go choose a small terracotta idol from the bazaar for the day that Ganesha "came to live" in our house for ten days on his birthday and it was my duty, as the child of the house, to make his royal umbrella. First, I cut a perfect circle from the cover of an old notebook. Then, a long, thin piece of wood was pierced and glued through its middle for the stem. Then the whole thing had to be covered with crepe paper and toffee wrappers and a nice, neat fringe had to be added. I did my best but did not always get it just right.'

'However, Ganapati is the special god of children, and so my crooked umbrella was ceremonially presented to him. It was such a nice feeling to see my present to him there in the puja. It stayed over him for all ten days until the day of Visarjan, when we took his mud idol to a lake nearby and gently put it in the water to dissolve back into Nature. My mother made mountains of salt and sweet modaka at home for his birthday. She made an extra batch to give to poor children outside the neighbourhood temple where we went every Monday. These steamed or fried rice-flour dumplings had two versions; one with a salted lentil filling, and the other with a sweet filling of coconut and jaggery,' said the grandmother.

'It sounds delicious,' said the mother. 'I love Ganapati. I need his picture or a little statue of him around me always, to feel established and secure about where I am. I couldn't really bear it otherwise, could you? Looking out at the world, I mean, with its deliberate cruelties? Ganapati is my best and truest anchor in such a world and I feel I know exactly why our people chose him to be a god. Scholars can theorize all they like that we were afraid in the old days of wild elephants destroying our crops and so we "propitiated" them. I don't think those scholars come from elephant countries. They didn't grow up with a culture of elephant-whisperers and perhaps they couldn't understand our natural attraction. We admired and respected elephants and so it's not surprising to me today that Ganapati is a noble and good-natured presence in our lives.'

'I didn't know you had such strong feelings about Ganapati,' said the father, surprised.

'You know I lived in Mumbai where Ganapati is respected by almost everybody,' said the mother. 'So I was devastated on a visit to Chennai when I was about eight, to see a bunch of men, their lungis at half-mast above their knees, actually blocking a roadside shrine to Ganapati. The lungied men stopped people from laying down their offerings at the foot of Ganapati's granite idol. They were such nice offerings of red hibiscus, coconut and bananas, and Ganapati's noble head shone lustrously black from the oil of a million worshippers' lamps. But the men had wounding words ready for him instead.'

'Their leader sang loudly,

Andha Ganapatikku
Tondi peruthavidam
Eppadiyenraal . . .

And the rest chorused,

Kolakattey thinnadinaley
Anney, Anney!'

'It means, "Ganapati's paunch got so big . . . from eating modaka, brother, brother!"'

'How do you remember that when you don't speak the language?' said the guru, deeply interested.

'My local ayah had taken me there. She told me the meaning and taught me the words, I insisted on knowing. I've never forgotten it. Their sneering words hurt me so much that I started crying. Surely Ganapati would burst out of his idol, ears flaring and trunk raised, to crush them underfoot? But no, not one flower did he bother to drop from the garland around his neck. Instead, he stared benignly into the middle-distance. My ayah produced a hanky and wiped my face.'

'The men, who were part of the "rationalist" political movement out there grew tired because once they were done jeering, they had nothing more to say. The most memorable thing, though, is how the people who had come to pray to Ganapati stood aside and waited. My ayah told me they were just regular, everyday people who went to work, to pull a rickshaw, unload a ship at the harbour, sit at a desk or stand over a stove.'

'They didn't shout back. All they did was to move into the cool, pungent shade of a neem tree nearby and stand there without moving, waiting for the men to stop shouting and go away. They drew together, carefully holding their offerings of flowers, fruit and coconut. They were silent, patient and calm—and monumental like an elephant. They became like an elephant in their strength and silence. They waited for nearly half an hour without saying a word and so did my ayah and I, watching the drama.'

'I saw that those who loved him really loved him. People could say anything to Ganapati and he was good about it. He was fond and forgiving. That's why the regular people were there, to say hello nicely with little offerings; and they did not go away until they were done greeting him. They made a long, well-behaved line to get their turn face-to-face with Ganapati and silently tell him whatever they had come to say.'

'I thought that Ganapati was just like a mother—kind, protective and solving all your problems. Mothers could die—you know mine did when I was thirteen. Suddenly, just like that, she was gone and I never saw her again. But the elephant god didn't go anywhere. I understood that he never would, that he was deeply rooted in the soil. He couldn't talk to me like my mother had or brush my hair or hold me and tell me stories or sing me to sleep. But he was always there, and I could talk to him. I knew sweet little songs about him and little prayers to say every morning and evening and at his shrines. I could see him on the road, at the temple, at the zoo. I knew I could see him in the jungle, too, if only someone would take a little girl there. And I could always read stories about elephants.'

The child drew close and the grandmother leaned across to pat the mother's hand.

'I feel I was there with you,' she said softly to her daughter-in-law. 'Speaking of Shiva has made us share these things.'

'The very first elephant film I remember seeing was *Hatari!*,' said the father, to give his wife a moment to compose herself. 'It came out much before my time but they had a special screening at my school because it was interesting for children'.

'Like you, I saw it at a special screening, sitting between my father and his sister at my father's club,' responded the mother, appreciating his cue. 'My aunt was nice to me but I was a bit afraid of my father, who was very tall and very short-tempered. "Hatari" means danger in Swahili and the film began with a terrifying chase after a rhino by American actors playing wildlife catchers.'

'The hero was John Wayne, and the heroine, Elsa Martinelli, played a photographer. They had an argument when she suddenly turned up to photograph his adventures,' said the father.

'But it took a long time for the scenes with the baby elephants to appear and I squeaked, "When will the elephants come?"' said the mother, laughing now. 'My father sternly told me to shut up, and I was frightened into silence at once. My aunt whispered that I had to wait for the elephants. Soon, three little baby elephants got adopted by the heroine and she led them to the pool for a bath with such a funny, bouncy tune playing that I promptly forgot about being afraid. It was the "Baby Elephant Walk", and I thought Ganapati would have loved it. There were many Indians in that film, it was shot in Tanganyika, which is now part of Tanzania. The shops and streets looked just like those in India and nobody seemed afraid of those three little elephants running around town.'

'Then, my friend's mother took me to see the Walt Disney film *Dumbo*, the story of the flying elephant and I felt very sorry for Dumbo through his troubles. I loved the song "Pink Elephants on Parade". I was so surprised later when other people told me that they were scared by that hallucinatory song. "But it's about elephants!" I said, and completely failed to see that it could be disturbing for some.'

'I want to see *Hatari!* and *Dumbo*,' said the child.

'You will. We'll watch it together,' said her father. 'And maybe we'll eat modaka again.'

'We should revive the custom, Ma,' said the mother. 'I've always been too busy at school and college and work and getting married and being a mom myself to learn to make modaka. But you described it so well that I'm suddenly inspired to learn.'

'I would love to show you, it's quite easy. A no-fuss treat for a no-fuss god who doesn't need grand temples. He's perfectly at home anywhere you want him—on your desk or out by the road, under a tree or by a little village pond,' said the grandmother, eyes twinkling.

'I want to learn, too,' said her son.

'Me, too! I want to learn to make an umbrella and modaka for Ganapati, both,' said the child.

'Project Ganesh Chaturthi is announced,' said the grandfather. 'How did we let this nice festival to this very nice god lapse from our lives? Will you really make modakas? Our son's childhood comes back to me, thinking of them. My own childhood comes back.'

'And mine,' put in the guru with a droll look.

'Done!' said the mother, laughing, and they got up to wash their hands for dinner.

5

Malai Mandir

The family, which had had much to think about all week and put a project on track for Ganapati's birthday some months away, waited eagerly for Monday to bring the guru back. The modaka lessons had successfully begun, and the mother had made a fresh batch with sweet filling for the guru's visit. It was the first batch she had made on her own and she looked forward to giving the guru a rightful share of her experiment.

But the guru, whom they could normally set their clock by, was unaccountably late.

The family grew restless, waiting for him.

'Should we watch TV while we wait?' said the father, fiddling with the remote.

'No, let's not watch TV, please! It will disturb our minds and spoil our satsang mood,' protested the mother.

'Have you called him?' the grandmother asked the grandfather.

'I have, but his phone is out of range,' said the grandfather.

'No message from him? Nothing on WhatsApp?' asked the grandmother anxiously.

'Not a word, it's so unlike him,' worried the grandfather.

'Let's pray while we wait, it will calm us down and do him good if he's in trouble,' said the mother, inspired.

'A very good idea! In fact, why don't you sing a bhajan for us? I often hear you humming or singing the child to sleep but when have we last sat together like this with an opportunity to hear you?' said the grandmother, smiling.

'Oh, I would like that. There's a song that's been buzzing in my head all day for no reason I can think of except that it's satsang today,' said the mother with delicacy, not wanting to call a devotional song an 'earworm'.

She sat down on the carpet, facing them all, and launched into the song *Sheesh Gang Ardhang Parvati*, singing it in the slow, meditative style of Pandits Rajan and Sajan Mishra, not in the fast-paced *harati* or prayer style. The song described Shiva as half-Parvati with the Ganga flowing from his head, sitting serenely on Mount Kailash, surrounded by his companions amidst heavenly music played by celestials with birdsong adding more music while the sun and moon humbly adored him.

The mother's sweet, steady voice sang the beautiful Hindi words with such sincerity and conviction that the family's heart leapt in sudden joy, as though it, too, was present in that delightful gathering amidst the silvery snow mountains. The father and child looked as adoringly at the mother as the sun and the moon looked at Shiva in the song, while the grandparents blinked their suddenly misting eyes. They were a good-natured family on the whole but the day had brought some wear and tear to each one, which had made them uneasy and a little cross while waiting for the guru. The song made them feel well and happy again and they heard it with gratitude for the mother's talent.

Just as the mother finished the song, even before the family could come out of its spell, the door bell rang. The father sprang up to open the door and found the guru there, holding a fan of peacock feathers and a fragrant twist of paper.

'I'm so sorry I'm late, and I forgot to charge my phone,' said the guru when he was ushered in.

'Thank God you're here now. We were worried,' said the grandmother as everyone got up to greet him.

'It's been a very exciting day for me. I spent both the morning and the afternoon at Uttara Swami Malai.'

'Do you mean the Malaai Mandir?' said the father.

'Yes, it's named after the famous old Kartikeya temple at Swami Malai in Tamil Nadu. "Malai" means "hill" in Tamil. The "a" is short in both places, so it's "malai", not "malaai", which is our word for cream. We call it "Malai Mandir" locally. That's like saying "Hill Temple", a happy union of Tamil and Hindi, which is perfect since Kartikeya's temples are usually found on a hill top,' said the guru.

'What took you there today on two visits? Was it because temples are usually shut in the afternoon?' said the grandfather.

'That's right. I went back at four o'clock when they reopened for evening service. Since I'd planned to tell you about Kartikeya this evening, I thought it would be nice to spend the day there, thinking of him. I saw the elegant puja they did in the morning service. And a while ago, I saw Kartikeya's idol with the chandan kaapu or covering of sandalwood paste. When the priest waved the *harati* fire at him, his face seemed alive! It was so beautiful. I've brought you all some holy ash from there, a proper Shaiva prasad. And I couldn't resist getting this little peacock feather fan for you from the hawkers outside, because Kartikeya's mount is the peacock,' said the guru, handing the pretty fan to the child.

'Thank you, Teacher,' said the child, doing a namaste to the guru and a little dance step, waving the fan. 'Kartikeya is far from home here, isn't he?'

Just then, the mother brought in modaka, chakli and tea for the guru. 'Let Guruji taste a modaka first,' she smiled. When the modaka had been duly praised, a crisp, sesame-sprinkled chakli eaten and a cup of restorative tea drunk, the guru fished in his kurta's front pocket and produced a little laminated 'calendar god' picture of Kartikeya as a bright-faced little boy.

He looked a bit like the 'Murphy baby' in old calendars from the twentieth century, rosy, plump and smiling, with curly hair. He had holy ash smeared in the three stripes of Shiva across his forehead with a bright red tilak in the middle. He wore gold earrings and tightly held a little golden *vel* or spear in his chubby fist. The spear represented his mother Parvati, the Shakti or super-strength that he would need later as a warrior.

'Another good friend for you,' said the guru, giving the pleasant picture to the child. 'Kartikeya as a little boy is a special god for children, like his elder brother Ganapati. They are the best of friends, those two, though Kartikeya has a bit of a temper and can fly off in a rage on his peacock whereas nothing can rattle big brother Ganapati. Together, they make a great team and look out for each other. Many children like to think of them as their elder brothers. And how Kartikeya likes that! Since he's a younger brother himself. He loves people who like to read and write and he absolutely loves poetry. He's also a warrior in his grown-up form, a tough one. In fact, Sri Krishna says of his own best qualities in the Bhagavad Gita, in Chapter Ten, Verse 24, "*Senaninam Aham Skanda* (Of generals, I am Skanda)", Skanda being yet another name for Kartikeya.'

'Besides little Krishna, Kartikeya is the other boy-god that people love to love, especially in the south. But do you know that Kartikeya was once widely worshipped across the plains of north and east India, and in Himachal Pradesh, Uttarakhand and Kashmir? Old sculptures and texts tell us so. He was once the favourite god of the warlike clans of Haryana and Punjab, the Yaudheyas. A branch of the Yaudheyas, called the Maha Mayurakas, had champion horsemen and horse breeders in what is now Rohtak and regions nearby in Haryana. It says so in the *Mahabharata*, in the section called the Rajasuya Parva. "Rohitka" as Rohtak was once known, was apparently Kartikeya's favourite city in the plains. Even ancient Buddhist texts talk about Kartikeya's popularity in the north.'

'So Kartikeya actually came home when he came to Uttara Swami Malai? Imagine that!' said the father.

'Yes, that's what he did, after many centuries. Until Uttara Swami Malai was consecrated in 1973, there was not a single temple to Kartikeya to be found in the north except for one at Pehowa near the Punjab-Haryana border, where Kartikeya is a bachelor god, and one at Chamba in Himachal Pradesh. Women are not allowed at the Pehowa temple. Perhaps the turbulent history of that region was a reason.

'Whereas Uttara Swami Malai has become so holy that it's now accepted as the seventh chakra, the Sahasrara Kshetra that completes the circuit of six ancient, powerful "chakra temples" to Kartikeya in the south. That's another story. Today, there are temples to Kartikeya around the world . . . I counted Sri Lanka, Malaysia, Singapore, Indonesia, Australia, New Zealand, Switzerland, UK, USA and Canada.'

'However, it's quite miraculous how his temple in Delhi came to be. Kartikeya or Kumar, "the young boy", as we also call him, came back to the north in a most extraordinary way,' said the guru.

6

Kumar

'First, we need to recall what we know about Kartikeya's circumstances,' said the guru to his expectant audience. 'Before him, Ganapati was born of Parvati's body. One day, while bathing, she scrubbed herself with many scented herb powders and from the foam and scurf on her limbs she suddenly thought to make the image of a little boy and she did. He looked so sweet that she impulsively breathed life into him and there he was, her little son Ganesh. But Kartikeya was born very differently. He shot out in six sparks from Shiva himself, from the all-destroying *netragni*, the fierce fire in Shiva's third eye, on his forehead.'

'Ganapati was created by Parvati's whim and became a universal darling, the embodiment of luck, learning and mystic power. He was made the first god to be prayed to before starting anything. That was by Shiva's order. But Kartikeya's birth has a backstory stretching all the way to the oldest tales about Shiva. Listen carefully as I try to tell it step by step, before I tell you the saga of Malai Mandir, the first new temple to Kartikeya in the north.'

'Very long ago, Brahma the Creator was given the task of making people inhabit the three worlds, which were well-connected to each other then. I've already told you about the three races he created for Svarg, Bhulok and Patal. For Bhulok, the earth, Brahma first created four handsome young men to be the ancestors of mankind and they sat down to pray for guidance on the shore of Manasarovar. Suddenly, a great white swan swam up before them.'

'It was Shiva, the ultimate free soul or "supreme swan", the Paramahamsa. The swan swam all over the lake to warn the four young men that the world was merely maya or illusion, and that the only way to escape its bonds was to refuse to become fathers. Shiva did that because he felt that it was only fair to warn them that creation was just a game for the gods. The young men got the message and serenely continued to meditate by the lake, and for all we know, they may be there still, invisible to the human eye, Sanat, Sanandan, Sanatan and Sanat Kumar, eternally youthful and lost in the ecstasy of meditation.'

'Shiva warned us, too, and still warns us by wearing ash, *vibhuti*. By doing this, he silently tells us that that is what it all comes down to ultimately, so don't fall for the illusion that'll be around you always. Don't waste your time on earth just eating, sleeping, gossiping and shopping, pleasantly though it passes the time, it's not worth it. Life is too short to waste in being mean to others. Instead, use your time to be nice to others, especially to those who need help, to wipe out karma from your past lives.'

'Whether we listen to Shiva's message or not, those first four beings certainly did. Brahma saw that they had eluded him. He then breathed out and the sage Narada appeared who too wished to stay single like the four youths, for he wanted to be free to travel the three worlds. Brahma shrugged, blessed Narada and sent him on his way. He next created eight great lords with many powers, strong tastes and big egos. They were the mighty Prajapatis and it was they who let loose the six evil passions into the world that infected the three worlds forever.'

'These negative qualities are called the Shad Ripu or Six Enemies who destroy us from within. They are *kama*, lust; *krodha*, anger; *lobha*, greed; *moha*, attachment; *mada*, pride; and *matsarya*, jealousy. They prevent us mortals from attaining *moksha* or salvation, which is what Shiva had warned the four handsome youths about.'

'To provide men and women to populate the earth that the Prajapatis were sent to rule, Brahma created the first man, Manu, and the first woman, Shatarupa, who created many children.'

'The chief of the Prajapatis was Daksha. He disliked Shiva because he felt that Shiva had not been respectful enough to him on an occasion. That was just Daksha's vanity since Shiva was far greater than he. Daksha took an indecent pride in his wealth and luxurious lifestyle, living in a grand palace, eating off gold plates and wearing precious gems. He made fun of Shiva for dressing simply, for living by himself out in the woods and for having friends from all walks of life. But it didn't matter to Shiva if you were pretty, rich or talented. Rather, he had a soft spot for the lame ducks of the world—the damaged, the broken, the worried, the weeping, the frightened, the sick and the lonely. He liked those people best who had clean hearts and clean minds, innocent of guile.'

'If Shiva has one weakness, it's water—*abhishekha priyo Shiva*. Shiva loves the feel of flowing water and is usually to be found bathing in a lake or river, when not lost in meditation in some icy Himalayan cave or dancing for fun with the goblins in the cremation ground. His best companion is his mount, the gigantic bull, Nandi, who guards him fiercely and the snakes that he shelters on his tall, strong and pale body.'

'Daksha was married to haughty, beautiful Prasuti, a daughter of Manu and Shatarupa, and had sixteen lovely daughters himself. Daksha was very proud of them and called them "princesses of the blood" as though he were the monarch of the three worlds. Sati, his youngest child, his pet, caught a glimpse of Shiva while out on a picnic with her sisters. After that she couldn't stop thinking of him in secret. When Daksha set up Sati's swayamvar, or marriage-by-choice, she was brought into the great hall of the palace to look at the line-up of rich, clever men whom Daksha had invited as would-be bridegrooms. Sati was expected to choose one of them as her husband. She had to put the flower garland she held around his neck. But Shiva was nowhere in sight, because he had not been invited.'

'In despair, Sati flung her garland into the air, crying, "If I am truly Sati, may Shiva receive this garland!" And suddenly, there stood Shiva, drawn by Sati's utter sincerity, with her garland around his neck. Daksha felt that Sati had thrown herself away disastrously but had no choice except to let her go with Shiva to his home on Mount Kailash.'

'This love story had a horrible end. Sati insisted on going to a special puja at Daksha's palace, although she and Shiva were not invited. You see, the only place you can really go to uninvited is a satsang, to hear katha and bhajan. In the old days, you could go uninvited to a friend's place, too. But not any more, life has got too busy, hasn't it? Shiva explained patiently to Sati that it was not correct to go uninvited, but Sati was used to having her way. She insisted on going and went on her own to Daksha's palace, leaving Mahadev behind on Kailash.'

'There, her father spoke so harshly and rudely about Shiva that Sati could not bear to hear his words and, rebuking Daksha, gave up her life then and there. Today we might wonder if it was a severe instance of "Takotsubo cardiomyopathy", or dying of a broken heart, a death caused by a rush of immense emotional or physical stress. Such a death is thought to happen by the toxic effects of stress hormones on the heart muscle and cardiac blood vessels. It is said to occur more in older women, but we can imagine the terrible rush of humiliation and grief that Sati must have felt, to be talked to like that in public by her father.'

'When Shiva was told, he furiously attacked Daksha, broke up the gathering and wrecked the place before disappearing with Sati's body flung over his shoulder.'

'Shiva's fury and sorrow plunged the whole world into deep gloom. To save the situation, Vishnu repeatedly flung his discus at Sati's body. He cut it up into fifty-one pieces that fell on earth and became high-energy points called

Shakti Peeth, places of goddess-strength. The farthest one north-east is Kamakhya in Guwahati in Assam. The farthest one north-west is Hinglaj Devi in Balochistan. Since it's in a desert, which is called *maru* in Sanskrit, old holy texts call it Marutirtha Hinglaj, meaning "Hinglaj, the shrine in the desert".'

'Feeling the weight gone, Shiva retreated into a remote mountain cave, vowing never to marry again but to meditate forever.'

'A tragic story,' mourned the grandfather. 'My heart breaks for Shiva and Sati Dakshayini.'

'Yes, there can be no other opinion on it. But we have to take the rough with the smooth,' said the guru.

'But, Guruji, you yourself can't bear the thought of the Uttara Kanda in the Ramayana,' said the grandfather. 'Not that I can. I've felt bad about it since I was a boy.'

'Ah, you've got me there,' sighed the guru. 'I go to pieces thinking of it. Nor will anybody who gives religious discourses touch it. They can't bear to. Nor could the audience listen without weeping aloud. It's too harrowingly out of character for Rama, and as for Sita, the injustice kills us. It's the saddest love story in the world that we simply cannot resist for so many reasons. Well, I suppose that's why the epics keep us so deeply attached. We take it all very personally because the gods are so real to us. I've met people who know much more about Sri Rama's family than their own.'

'Anyhow, let's proceed to Part Two. With Shiva lost to the world, the forces of darkness in Patal cautiously began to emerge. They were terrified of Shiva, for not only had he drunk up the terrible Kalakuta in one swallow but had also killed many over-ambitious asuras who had won amazing boons by the force of their *tapas* or austerities, like standing on one leg for years amidst five fires, not eating anything, giving up even water and finally, living only on air. The *Shiva Purana* has the gory details of how demon after demon was destroyed by Shiva. He is called "Tripurantaka", the destroyer of three asura cities, after one such difficult labour.'

'Now, with Shiva having locked himself away, the asuras, although they themselves worshipped Shiva, felt that the coast was clear to take another shot at their favourite activity, which was to harass the devas. So the asura Surapadman and his brother Tarakan embarked on an absolutely horrendous *tapas* to coax a boon from Brahma. The old Creator could not bear it when his creatures hurt themselves; so *tapas* to him was emotional blackmail of a high degree. None of the gods could bear to see this, really, and Brahma was particularly susceptible, even more than Shiva who loved austerities and was easily touched if someone made a real effort. That, by the way, is why Shiva is called "Ashutosh", meaning "easily pleased". And just as unpredictably, he erupts in fury. *Kshane tushta, kshane rushta*: pleased one moment and angry the next. It can be an endearing trait, but it sometimes led to complicated lilas.'

'Having been denied immortality, all asuras who reached the boon-granting stage inevitably began by asking for eternal life. Brahma had to say no each time, for that was not in his power to give, but in Shiva's, Shakti's and particularly Vishnu's, who was known to be too shrewd to fall for asura tricks. So the asuras tried to get immortality from Brahma through indirect moves.'

'Surapadman and Tarakan came away from Brahma mighty pleased with their deal. The boon they had asked for and received was that nobody could kill them except a son of Shiva. That son had to be born only after Shiva was married but he could not be born of a female. This was so cunningly constructed that the asura brothers felt totally safe and promptly attacked Indralok, the home of the devas.'

'The devas fled to Brahma for sanctuary.'

'"Do something! Save us!" they wept.'

'"The first thing to do is get Shiva married. But who will marry him now?" said Brahma, annoyingly practical.'

'The devas thought hard.'

'"We can only throw ourselves on the mercy of Shakti, the feminine side of Shiva," they said nervously and began to pray to this multiple energy that could be many things all at once.'

'Shakti, who moved independently of Shiva although she was half of him, took pity on the devas. She willed herself to be born on earth, taking care to choose good parents who worshipped Shiva. She chose Himavan, lord of the snow peaks, and his soft-hearted wife, Mena, who were very happy with each other and thought it would be nice to have a child to hopefully add to their happiness. Accordingly, one day, Himavan found an exquisite baby girl asleep on a rare lotus that had mysteriously bloomed in icy Manasarover. He brought her home to Mena as bhagvat prasad, the blessed gift of the gods.'

'As the daughter of the mountains, Shakti was given the names Parvati and Girija, since "*parvat*" and "*giri*" mean "mountain". She played her part perfectly in this lila of her own making. She delighted her earthly parents by being a caring, affectionate child. She enjoyed an enchanted girlhood, and worshipped Shiva with all her heart right from when she was a very little girl. When she grew up, she tracked him down to his mountain cave and brought him water and his favourite *vilva* or bel leaves every day without fail. But Shiva never noticed.'

'The watching devas now thought of a way to make Shiva open his eyes, look at Parvati and fall in love with her. They recruited the services of Kama, the cheerful and confident young god of love, who alone feared nobody for almost every creature succumbed to his flowery love arrows. However, Kama quailed at the thought of committing the sin of *swami droham*, of doing something against God. But he was bound by his duty to Indra, his king, who gave him no choice. So Kama made up his mind to be brave, quietly consoling himself that if he had to risk dying, it was best to be killed by Shiva himself. Kama took along his wife Rati and his friend Vasant, the Spring, to make everything pretty and pleasant around Shiva when he opened his eyes and looked at Parvati.'

'When Parvati arrived and knelt in prayer, Kama shot his arrow with deadly accuracy at Shiva. Alas, it proved deadly for him instead, for Shiva's eyelids fluttered, he looked for the source of the disturbance, burnt poor Kama to ashes with a fiery look from his third eye and vanished! He did not look once at Parvati, who was left consoling a heartbroken Rati.'

'But Parvati was not a quitter. "I have to do this for the devas, so I shall," she told herself sternly and just as sternly, she told Shiva in her head, "You like austerity, do you? I'll show you austerity." Overcoming her parents' natural objections, Parvati decided to go deep into the forest to begin an unrelenting fast and prayer to win over Shiva since nothing else seemed likely to move him—not her beauty, not her youth, nor her royal parentage nor her sincere intent to marry him for a good cause.'

'Parvati put away her royal robes and put on the chira-valkala or hermit's habitual dress of tree-bark. She stood in the waters of a lonely pond, praying all day to Shiva, indifferent to heat, rain and cold, and to the very real threat from insects, reptiles, birds and animals. Her skin grew deeply tanned and her forehead, nose and chin were painfully sunburned, as were her shoulders and arms. Her hair grew matted like Shiva's, her body shrank and her delicate ribs stuck out as she gradually stopped eating. "*Aparna!*" said the shocked sages who passed by, "she doesn't eat even a leaf," while Mena, Parvati's mother, cried, "*Ooh, ma!* Oh, don't!" The stoic princess thus acquired the names Uma and Aparna.'

'The horrified devas watched helplessly as Parvati grew thinner and thinner and frailer and frailer, with no sign of giving up. "We're so sorry we did this to you, Mother," they wept in remorse from their safe house in Brahmalok. "Why won't Shiva *listen*?"'

'Oh!' said the child in distress, not meaning to interrupt but too deeply affected by Parvati's suffering to stay silent. 'Won't Shiva go to her soon? Poor Parvati!'

Her father hugged her, his own eyes suspiciously moist. 'Let's listen to some more to find out,' he said soothingly.

'We now come to the more obviously happy part of the story,' said the guru to the child. 'But I think Parvati's *tapas* was marvellous, too, because she was stretching her limits in her human form and just wouldn't give up. So far, I've more or less followed Parvati's story the way it's told in *the Kumarasambhavam, The Birth of Kartikeya*. This is an epic poem by Kalidasa from the fourth century.'

'Kalidasa took the story from Valmiki's *Srimad Ramayanam*, from the first book, the Bala Kandam, Sargas thirty-six and thirty-seven, in which Sage Vishvamitra, on the way to Videha, tells Rama and Lakshmana about the birth of Kartikeya. Valmiki also has a very touching scene where Rama's mother Kausalya calls down the grace of all the gods on him when he goes in exile for fourteen years. She begins with *Skandascha Bhagavan Devaha*, invoking Kartikeya.'

'Kalidasa is said to have lived in Ujjain, you know, where your grandfather took your father to see Shiva as Mahakaleshwar. Kalidasa must have seen that ancient shivling, too! Isn't that a thought? I hope you'll read the *Kumarasambhavam* yourself one day. There are eight thrilling verses in particular in which Kalidasa describes how Kama, peering from behind a rock, sees Shiva meditating in utter stillness on a tiger skin under a tree. Even the breeze does not dare to disturb him. Kama's weapons almost fall from his suddenly nerveless fingers in that great hush. Those verses make you feel that you actually see Shiva for yourself.'

'Is the poem in Sanskrit?' said the child, interested.

'Yes, it is. It's best to start learning Sanskrit as soon as possible, to get it right. Your prayer to Ganapati was well said, so I know you won't be frightened of Sanskrit. But it's hard work! You know, of course, that the English alphabet has twenty-six letters. Well, the Sanskrit alphabet has twice as many. We learn them in strings. If you learn Sanskrit properly, your mind will be so well-trained that you'll find many other subjects very easy, like language, law, math, poetry, logic and science.'

'Yes, we plan to give her that foundation,' said the mother. 'Her school is being pulled this way and that about teaching Sanskrit. So we've decided to find her a good teacher for lessons at home. I missed out, and I think it's too important for us to leave to chance. In fact, we wanted to ask you to recommend someone suitable . . . someone who loves both prose and poetry and can communicate that love to her.'

'Ah, *gadyam* and *padyam*, prose and poetry,' smiled the guru. 'I'll think of someone. There's a lovely poem in praise of Sanskrit for the many gifts it has given India . . . *subharati suramya*, "the language of our enchantment". No wonder Macaulay wanted to cut us off from it and turn us into brown Englishmen to serve the needs of Empire. But English also woke us up and sparked off Hindu reform, didn't it? We were dragged, kicking and screaming, into the modern world.'

'Anyhow, to resume our tale, Shiva did come by at last and marry Parvati in a grand wedding, with Parvati first making sure to restore Kama's spirit to Rati.'

'The best song I've ever heard about Shiva-Parvati's marriage is *Shivji bihane chale; palki sajai ke bhabhuti ramai ke, ho Ram* (Shivji is on his way to be married wearing holy ash, with a bridal palanquin). It's a storytelling classic. I enjoy the words, the music and the vivid picture it paints. You feel like you're right there, dancing with the happy crowd . . . *sang-sang barati chale dholva bajai ke ghorva daudai ke, ho Ram* (along with him is the bride-groom's party beating drums and speeding on horses).'

'*Shankar ka Vivah* (Shankar's wedding), we know it, too,' said the grandfather. 'The oral tradition remains as strong as ever in our mother tongues, thank God. That's what we're doing ourselves now, aren't we—katha in English?'

'*Shankar ka Vivah* is a brilliant katha,' said the father. 'You can hear different versions on YouTube with the full flavour of Bhojpuri!'

'I love that song,' said the mother. 'It makes me feel light and cheerful like I was a Shivagana myself . . . *suttva ghumaike, ghuttva lagaike, ho Ram* (Passing a pipe of weed around and taking a swig of bhang).' She lapsed into a giggling fit.

'Why does Shiva smoke and drink with the ganas?' said the child sternly, with a look at her convulsed mother. Her father put up his hand to hide a grin.

'Shiva does all that to show us how perfectly free he is, or so we fondly think,' said the guru. 'It's not a good idea for everyday life on earth, in case it gets too much and spoils our health. But there's nothing "wrong" with it for grown-ups socially, within limits, of course. It's a pitiful sight only when you see someone out of control. A true lady and a true gentleman know the art of self-control and how to moderate their behaviour. Mahadev certainly did. But his wild appearance upset those who lived by tight outward rules. He was beyond the understanding of many people. So, you see, Parvati really had a tough job. First convincing Shiva to marry her and then convincing Mother Mena to let her marry Shiva—this wild, ash-smeared yogi hung about with snakes and surrounded by tipsy, capering goblins. His only plus point was that he was a "bath freak" as we'd say back in the day. He bathed all the time.'

'But the wedding went off well. All three worlds were joyful witness. It was our first big party, with everyone present, and we still celebrate it. The wedding took place a day before the moonless night of Amavasya in the month of Phalgun, which is mid-February to mid-March by the Indian calendar. All over India and wherever we go, we celebrate it every year as Maha Shivratri, the great night of Shiva. Typically, we bathe and fast and go to the temple to offer Shiva bel leaves and water. That's what he likes as presents from us—cleanliness, an effort to detox, and most of all, loving remembrance.'

'It was a happy marriage, for Parvati was more emotionally mature than Sati. Shiva fell wholly in love with Parvati for her strength of character, and she with Shiva for the goodness and grandness of his nature. He was incapable of a pettiness. It became a splendid, deeply loving friendship between equals, spiced now and then by a quarrel or two, which was really just another round of lila or divine games, for this partnership was as knit as *vaak* and *arth*, as word and meaning, inseparable from each other. It was sturdily made of trust, loyalty and mutual appreciation, setting an example to the world.'

'Of course, the devas showed up soon after, begging Shiva to think of their unhappy situation as powerless exiles, and somehow produce a son who could liberate them from asura rule and enable them to go home to Indralok. All the devas assembled on Mount Kailash to piteously petition Shiva except Yama, god of Death, who was detained round the clock by Surapadman. The asura king kept Yama close by as his personal physician. With the Lord of Death himself as the doctor, which infection, disease or hurt could dare come near those he guarded?'

'Ah, but how the gods love to outwit the vain, the greedy and the presumptuous! Shiva heard the devas out and shot those six sparks of fire from his third eye, which landed in the Ganga. Ganga's waters hissed in pain for she couldn't bear the heat and she passed the fire on to Agni, the fire god, who himself found it too hot to handle. So he put the six sparks on six lotuses in a cool little forest pond surrounded by *saravana* or marshy reeds.'

'The six sparks, with their first force spent, instantly turned into six tiny baby boys so that the soft, delicate lotuses could hold them without being burnt. This lovely secret pond was where six beautiful star maidens came every evening to bathe. Together, they made up the constellation Krittika, also known as the Pleiades. The star maidens looked after the little boys until Shiva and Parvati came looking for them. Parvati was so happy that she held them all together in one big hug. This magically turned the six children into one lovely boy, Kumar. To thank the star maidens for looking after her child, Parvati said that she would also call him Kartikeya, meaning "of the Krittika".'

'Kumar grew from a toddler into the most wonderful boy. He led the devas into battle against the asuras Surapadman and Taraka. He won with the help of his father's blessings, his mother's strength and his own courage. Both asuras were crushed and begged for mercy. The *Skanda Purana* by Vyasa says that Kumar, being just a boy-god then, had ridden to battle on a sturdy goat with wickedly curved horns in remembrance of a dangerous wild goat that he had quelled on Kailash with his child's strength. When the two defeated asuras pleaded for grace, Kumar turned Surapadman into a peacock for his mount and placed Tarakan as a rooster on his war chariot's banner. Of the many birds on earth, these two look upwards to heaven to utter their calls.'

'The gods do not exclude sinners from their kindness if they sincerely repent. Whereas, a greedy, jealous person like Duryodhana in the Mahabharata disqualified himself from grace by staying arrogant to the end. He would not give even one needle-point of land to his cousins and plunged them all into war to become a *kulantaka*, the destroyer of his own clan.'

'Kumar was so bright and endearing that anyone who saw him took one look and doted on him at once. Well, just think of whose child he was. He had the priceless gift of charm and a strong streak of mischief. He loved to tease those who loved him, especially scholars and poets puffed up in their own importance, by appearing to them as a cheeky little boy or as an old man. At the same time, he was known to be very protective and loyal towards his devotees, which made generation after generation love him more and more and more. "You exist to make us live!" they cried.'

'Acharya Adi Shankara wrote a powerful thirty-three-verse Sanskrit poem to him that he composed at Kartikeya's temple at Tiruchendur on the Coromandel shore.

'Kumar is also called "Subrahmanya", so Acharya's poem is called the *Subrahmanya Bhujangam.* They say that the poem sprang out of a glowing vision that Acharya had of Kumar seated deep in his heart.'

'Acharya set it in Jagati Chhand, the twelve-syllable Vedic metre. When you say it aloud, the poem seems to glide forward like a snake on its "shoulders", which we call *bhujanga prayatam.* This poem is believed to cure us of physical, mental and spiritual sickness. So people recite it even today in Maharashtra, Goa, Karnataka, Andhra Pradesh, Telangana, Kerala and Tamil Nadu like how the *Hanuman Chalisa* is recited in the north, as a *kavach* or protective prayer. I'll tell you my favourite verse:

> 'Mayuradi roodam, Maha vaakya gudam
> Manohari devam, Mahatchitta geham
> Mahi Devadevam, Maha Vedabhavam,
> Mahadeva Balam, Bhaje Lokapalam'

'It says, "Who rides the peacock; who is the secret cave of truth in the hearts of believers; who is the lord of the celestials; who embodies knowledge; who is the Great God's son—Hail to that protector of the world."'

'There, I've tried to translate it, but it just doesn't compare with how it sounds in the original. Why not add this verse to the prayer you say to Ganapati? It's so easy to say aloud, unlike some jaw-breakers in Sanskrit. It's Acharya's gift of Kumar to us all, wherever we live.'

'The Tamil people in particular took Kumar wholly to their hearts. Indeed, they say he was always theirs. "You may stand like a stone in your temples but to us you are like a ripe fruit, the fruit of knowledge and mercy," they said. They called him "Murukan", "the beautiful one", and wrote reams of poetry about him that they still sing. Especially, they love the *Tiru Pugazh*, the poems to Kumar by the fifteenth-century poet Arunagiri Nathar. *Tiru Pugazh* means "Holy Praise" or "Divine Glory". Arunagiri compares the sight of Murukan on his peacock to the red sun rising on a blue-green sea.'

'The *Tiru Pugazh* became a companion book to the *Tevaram*, seven volumes of songs about Shiva from very ancient times. Imagine, there are hereditary singers of *Tevaram* even today at many old Shiva temples out south. Those songs have been sung from the seventh century! Today, many modern young people go to special classes to learn to sing both *Tiru Pugazh* and *Tevaram* with the stories and the "Shaiva Siddantha" or philosophy explained. Whatever else these young people may do in the world, Kumar and Shiva are alive to them in their daily life.'

'It is with these old stories and songs on their lips, and with the most dedicated love for Kumar and Shiva in their hearts, that a group of young men in their twenties came all the way north from Chennai in the winter of 1944 to work in the Government Secretariat. They were summoned because their English had become very good in the Madras Presidency where the British had been for nearly 300 years.'

'The British government of the day in Delhi knew about their language skills. But it's likely that it did not know of the divine love that burned in their youthful Indian hearts or what that love would make them do in far-off Delhi for their Murukan, their Kumaran, Kandan, Kartikeyan, Guhan, Subrahmanyan, Saravanan, Velayudhan . . . they had so many meaningful names for him. What's more, they carried an ancient *shadakshari* or six-syllable mantra with them, invoking his grace—*Saravana Bhava*—just as they carried the powerful *panchakshari* or five-syllable mantra for Shiva, *Namas Shivaya*.'

'I'll tell you the rest next Monday. I'll leave you with the thought that Kumar, born of Shiva's holy fire, is with you in your home as the light in every flame lit for worship— "*Deepa mangala jyoti namo namah* (I bow to the Light of every lamp lit for God)". That's what Arunagiri said of Kumar over 500 years ago.'

7

Shivaskanda Murti

'*Sri Parameshvara prityartham*,' said the guru in a ringing voice when he settled down to speak on his next visit. 'This is being done to please God.'

He surprised himself by saying so, for the words belonged in the act of *sankalpa* that described the when, where, why and what of a ritual that was about to start. It was a formal declaration, stating space and time, of your intention or goal before you began a puja, a pilgrimage or a worthy project.

'Perhaps I've begun to think of these sessions as a sacred rite,' he mused. 'And the words happen to be so apt for the story that I'm about to tell. Those young men and their successors in Delhi must have uttered these very words when they began to dream of the ambitious project of building a traditional temple in a strange, new city so far from home. But look at the underlying cultural unity of India. People in almost every region say these words when they ritually state their resolve to do something worthwhile—*Sri Parameshvara prityartham*.'

'Saying so is our brave human defiance of the fact that life flings so much sorrow at us . . . "*janma dukham, jara dukham, jaya dukham punah punah, samsara sagaram dukham, tasmat jagrata, jagrata*", like Adi Shankara said. "Birth is painful, old age is wretched; desire, never-endingly, is the source of misery and pain. This ocean of Samsara is full of grief. Therefore, wake up; wake up . . . to seek God." Acharya said that in his Proclamation of Detachment, the *Vairagya Dindima* . . .'

'Guruji,' said the grandfather gently. 'You're miles away.'

The guru came back with a little start. 'Sorry, I was thinking of Malai Mandir, and how it began with a song and a prayer.'

'Some of my colleagues say that it's better to give money in charity than to build or restore temples,' said the mother hesitantly.

'We're capable of both. Charity is our human duty. Remember Prajapati's watchword to us? *Datta*, give, be generous. Sometimes it may provide only temporary material relief, but it's still worth doing if it makes someone's life a little better. However, besides contributing to material charity, we are fully permitted to support the arts and to make a new temple or restore an old one—it is something more permanent for the emotional relief and cultural expression of many people, including ourselves,' said the guru. 'There's a nice saying, "If you have but two coins left, with one, buy food to feed your body and with the other, buy flowers to feed your soul."'

'That handful of young men in their twenties began to celebrate the Skanda Shashti festival from the year 1944 in New Delhi, gathering in one another's homes. Six years later, in 1950, as more and more people eagerly showed up for the puja, south Indians in Delhi who had formed a cultural society in 1949 called the Shanmukhananda Sangeeta Sabha, took over the celebration as a public event. The society was named after Kumar, for "Shanmukha" is another name for him, meaning "six faces" after the six little boys looked after by the Krittika star maidens.'

'As word spread of these celebrations, a devotee who was an industrialist and philanthropist from Patna offered to pay for a metal icon of Kumar for worship and for the cost of taking it out in a procession each year at the end of the puja. But there was no proper place for daily puja to the icon.'

'The devotees began to dream of building a temple to Kartikeya. They looked for a suitable hillock, for that was where his temples were usually made out south—at places like Swami Malai, Palani, Tirutani, Tirupurankunram—"kunram" means hill, like "malai"—and Pazha Mudhir Cholai. Only the great temple of Tiruchendur, marking the place where Kartikya defeated Surapadman, is on the seashore.'

'Actually, there are many lovely temples all over south India to Kumar but these six make a special pilgrim circuit. Do you know that men and boys wear green dhotis when they go on this pilgrimage for Kumar? It's like how women and girls wear red for the Parvati circuit. Many male devotees carry a *kavadi* for Kartikeya. This is similar to the *kavad* or bamboo pole carried by the *kavadiya* pilgrims of north India.'

'These six temples mark the important events in Kartikeya's story.'

'He taught his father Shiva the meaning of the ultimate mantra, the Pranava or "Om" at Swami Malai.'

'He took off as a hermit to Palani while very young because he once mistakenly thought that his parents loved Ganapati better.'

'He defeated Surapadman at Tiruchendur.'

'He was married to Indra's daughter, Devasena, at Tirupurankunram, as an official reward for having won.'

'He withdrew to Tirutani to cool down from the heat of battle and won over the mortals by wooing and marrying Valli, the pretty daughter of a local tribal chieftan, Nambi. He had found Valli on the ground as a baby, like Janaka found Sita.'

'Kumar then appeared in glory with Valli and Devasena at Pazha Mudhir Cholai.'

'The story goes that Devasena and Valli were two mortal sisters, Amudavalli and Sundaravalli, who loved Mahadev and Parvati so much that they longed to be part of their family forever. They prayed very hard to Vishnu to be never separated and to marry a son of Mahadev, and so they got their wish.'

'Inspired by Parvati's fast for Shiva, the elder sister prayed and fasted all day, every day, and was reborn as the celestial princess Devasena, daughter of Indra. The younger sister, a light-hearted, fun-loving girl, prayed only during puja time. She loved playing all day in the forests and by the rivers, and so she was given human rebirth as Valli, a child of the woods. Beautiful, docile Devasena was married to Kumar first. But Valli, whose name means "creeper", though she was not a clinging, meek person at all, took some wooing! Kumar had to work hard to win her. Her story is one of the most ancient love stories in India.'

'One day, Narada saw Valli guarding a field of ripening *thinai* or foxtail millet from wild birds, armed with a slingshot. She cried "*Aalo -lam!*" as she expertly and gracefully swung it. She looked so pretty, confident and bright that Narada went to Tirutani nearby, where Kumar was cooling off from battle, to tell him about her. "Just the right sort for a young warrior," said Narada. Intrigued, Kumar went to see Valli in human disguise as a handsome hunter chasing a deer, and playfully tried to charm her. But she did not recognize him in human form. She wouldn't even look at the stranger for her heart was firmly fixed on Kumar in his godly form.'

'Kumar went away and reappeared as an old man to Valli's father Nambi Raja, who told her to look after the guest. It was a beautiful day, so Valli thoughtfully took her father's elderly guest out for a gentle walk in her beloved woods. She gave him wild honey and millet porridge to eat, and fetched him water in a wooden cup. She talked and laughed merrily and walked with a youthful spring in her step. Kumar was so smitten by this delightful girl that he forgot which disguise he was in and tried to hold her hand which she furiously knocked away in disgust. He had to telepathically ask big brother Ganapati to appear as a wild elephant and frighten Valli into his arms. She forgave him

only when the truth came out, that Kumar was in fact the
bridegroom that she herself wanted.'

'At a deep level, philosophers and yogis think of these
six temples as chakra points of kundalini energy.'

'I'll try to explain "kundalini" and "chakra" to you
separately with a diagram another time,' the guru broke off
to say to the child. 'These are terms from yoga philosophy
about the spiritual energy that every person has inside
them. Let's follow the Kartikeya story for now.'

'These six temples drew many saints and sages, who
often composed hymns about them. So such temples are
celebrated among the *paadal petra sthalam*, "places that
inspired song". See how faith is so deeply embedded in the
geography of India? North to south, east to west, almost
every square kilometre has the memory of a temple and the
memory of those who came to it. The dust of millions of
pilgrims' feet is mingled in our soil.'

'Well, in 1961, some devotees happened to notice a
small hillock on the then outskirts of Delhi, in what later
became the neighbourhood called Ramakrishnapuram.
You must try to imagine it as the wild scrubland and jungle
that it was in those days. Soon after spotting that hillock,
one of the devotees had a strange dream. He dreamt that
as he was going home from work, an old man suddenly
appeared by the road and timidly stopped him.'

'"Please will you walk me to my home? I feel dizzy and
I'm afraid of falling down," he said in a weak voice. The
old man looked so frail and pathetic that the young man
readily agreed to escort him home. The old man took him
to the foot of the very hillock that he and his friends had

spotted at a distance a few days back and pointed to its summit. "Thank you so much. That's my home up there," he said in a suddenly strong voice and vanished from sight. The devotee woke up from the dream at this point.'

'He told his core group of fellow-devotees about it the next day, and they agreed that it was a very good omen of divine will. As soon as they could, they rushed to inspect the hillock, scrambling up past rocks and thorn bushes, since there was no pathway. On the top, they found the scattered remains of an old stone structure. They asked a very senior friend in the archaeological survey office to check the old maps and he discovered that the hillock was marked "RP", meaning "religious place".'

'The ruins had an interesting tale attached to them. Local legend had it that there had once been an ancient temple to Shiva there from the days of the Mahabharata. Over thousand years ago, a local chieftan called Surajmal wanted to build a hilltop rest house for himself on that very spot and had the first load of stones brought up for construction. But his father had a dream about the prior existence of the old shivala or temple on that hill, and persuaded his son to stop building, which he did. So a dream disallowed that building and a thousand years later, another dream endorsed the making of another building, but this time, a temple. This is how the gods play with us.'

"'So Shiva is already there!" cried the astonished devotees when told of this history. "And after all these centuries, we seem directed to bring Kartikeya to that very spot. That sounds like Swami Malai, father and son together." Something deeper than they could understand was going on. Some ancient pattern encoded in the soil seemed to be talking to them. What, next?'

'The young men, who were somewhat older by now, boldly applied for the land which the authorities agreed to allot to them for Rs 25,000 if they formed a registered society. With the paperwork done, the devotees began the arduous task of fundraising.'

'The south Indian community in Delhi shared a deep love for Kartikeya across the states. The *Skanda Purana*'s Sahyadri Kand says that Kartikeya killed the asura Taraka in the hills of south Karnataka, and dipped his bloodstained spear in the river Dhara to cleanse it. This is in present-day Dakshin Kannada district, and the river is now called Kumaradhara. I've driven through this lush, beautiful region, and I still remember how it radiated peace and holiness.'

'It is here that we find the Kukke Subrahmanya temple that Sachin Tendulkar famously went to for Nagpuja. Adi Shankara had memorably stopped and prayed at the Kukke Subrahmanya temple during his great tour of India by foot.'

'I'm told *kukke* means cave, from old Kannada *kukshi* which is *guha* in Sanskrit and *gufa* in Hindi. A legend goes that Vasuki, Lord Vishnu's serpent, was once being chased by Garuda and sought refuge in Subrahmanya.'

'So while he's worshipped as a handsome young man in Tamil Nadu, many temples in Andhra Pradesh and Karnataka personify Kartikeya as a serpent, while at Tirupati, he is supposed to be the "snake-hill" of Seshachalam itself.'

'With so much history and feeling driving them, the south Indian community in Delhi, which was not rich in those days, saved and scraped and even sold off rings, chains and bangles, to somehow collect the money, and the land was bought.'

'But how were they to build the temple, that too, a traditional one to Kartikeya? Those days, nobody in Delhi knew how to make an appropriately carved, old-style temple in hard black granite. Their fingers had forgotten how after so many centuries. The devotees were keen to showcase Kumar with all his history. They wanted to link the long continuity of his tradition to the site of the ancient Shiva temple on the hill. So it would have to be made in south India and assembled in Delhi.'

'It was totally beyond the dreamers' means, involving tonnes of granite, heavy transport costs from the far south, an army of traditional stone carvers or *stapathi*, building a proper pathway to the top of the hill and deciding on the precise nature of the idol, which only a gifted master craftsman could make.'

'A proper temple also involved public facilities, with water and electricity bills, a roster of cleaning staff, basic accommodation and salaries for priests, money for musicians, singers and musical instruments, suppliers of flowers and *samagri* or ingredients for daily worship, puja items in silver, brass lamps and giant bells, a community hall and a kitchen to make the daily offering of *neivedyam* or consecrated food to share with devotees, prayer books, and a solid corpus fund for maintenance costs . . . it was overwhelming. Only kings and rich merchants could afford to build and endow such temples. How could modestly salaried, middle-class people dare to dream of such a grand project?'

'The young men prayed to Shiva and Parvati for guidance by meditating on the powerful Tamil hymn *Veyuru-tholi pangan* composed by the seventh-century boy-saint Sambandar. If you put it in English, it goes:

Who is half of bamboo-shouldered (tender-limbed) Parvati,
Whose throat is dark from drinking poison,
Who plays a faultless lute and wears on His head the
blemish-less moon and the Ganga,
Who has stolen into my heart,
Wherefore, without reserve, the Nine Planets always do
    good to us,
Who love the Lord.'

'Then, the answer occurred to them all: Go to Kanchipuram.'

'They coordinated their leave and went south by train on the cheapest berths. The only direct train from Delhi to Madras was the Grand Trunk Express (GT), introduced in 1929, which had the longest waiting list for any train in Indian Railways. In the 1960s and '70s, the 'GT' took over forty-two hours one-way to cross 2,186 km across the long length of our land past mountain ranges and mighty rivers like the Krishna and Godavari.'

'From Madras, or Chennai as it was later called, it was an hour's journey by bus to the old temple town of Kanchipuram, whose presiding deity was Parvati as Kamakshi, the "love-eyed goddess".'

'Their mission: to find out what the 68th Shankaracharya, head of the ancient religious institution called the Kamakoti Matt, had to say.'

'This was the luminous personality called Sri Chandrasekharendra Sarasvati, fondly known as "Paramacharya" and "Mahaperiyava", great teacher and great elder. Born to a Kannada-speaking family that had settled in the Tamil region, he lived for a hundred years between 1894 and 1994.'

'As a schoolboy, he won first prize for Bible studies and played the part of Prince Arthur in his school's production of Shakespeare's play, *King John*. Besides being fluent in English, he spoke many languages like Kannada, Telugu, Tamil, Malayalam, Hindi and Sanskrit. Nobody could figure out how he had acquired so many skills nor how he could converse so knowledgeably with visitors on any topic under the sun, even on aerodynamics, medicine and architecture, for he had been virtually kidnapped as a boy of thirteen and made into a sanyasi and head of the institution.'

'He had been taken away for some years to Mahendra Mangalam, a remote rural hideout by the river Kaveri, where learned pundits taught him the Vedas and Shastras. So how did he know so much else? And how was he able to predict what would happen in such-and-such a case or know exactly who, in a vast crowd, had stolen something out of sight at the back? He remains one of the mysteries of our age, connecting the old and the new India.'

'Gandhi met him in a cowshed in Pallaseni village in Palghat, Kerala, in 1929. Gandhi skipped his dinner, which he would not eat after 6 p.m., to carry on talking with the sage, who was much younger. The sage, in turn, wore only khadi after meeting Gandhi and discarded forever the old finery, like gold pendants, that he had been made to wear for big pujas as a religious head. In any case, the sage slept on bare ground and ate the most frugal food, while making sure to somehow feed thousands of people, particularly the poor, of any caste or creed.'

'The Dalai Lama called him "the monk of the century" for such was the Kanchi seer's spiritual power, knowledge and austerity. He also had an irresistible sense of humour and drew the most unlikely admirers without doing a thing to attract them—Indira Gandhi, Queen Frederika and Princess Irene of Greece, savants and scholars from Japan, South-east Asia, Iran, Europe and America, and hordes of Indian people, from canteen boys to kings. Presidents of India, cabinet ministers and chief ministers of huge Indian states flocked to him as well. He went around India on foot like Adi Shankara, visiting holy places and drawing large crowds wherever he went. He had a keen, piercing gaze that powerfully affected many people.'

'Everyone came to the humble cowshed or tree or riverside where this guru was frequently to be found camping. Quite often, they forgot what they had come to say for they were struck dumb by the kindness and lustre he radiated, and were content to stare. It was common for strangers to burst into tears when they saw him, for their masks fell off with just one look at that spiritual colossus. Many devotees declared that Sri Chandrasekharendra Sarasvati was Shiva himself, come amidst us to restore society's better values, save old temples and temple arts, indeed, save religion and culture from being lost in the colonial and post-colonial confusion.'

'The Kartikeya devotees in Delhi were familiar with the Kanchi seer's reputation, and had not only heard him discourse in Chennai but also regularly read his views on religion as reported in newspapers and magazines. Even atheists and people of other creeds respected him, for while he worked unceasingly to serve his faith, he had absolutely no hatred for or quarrel with anyone but instead, preached a life code of cultural and religious harmony.'

The guru stopped to retrieve a printout that was tucked into a book in his cloth bag. 'I found this on the internet. It's a translation of the Kanchi seer's summary in the 1960s of the stories that I have just told you about Parvati and Shiva,' he said, and putting on his glasses, began to read from the printout:

'Why did Kamakshi make Dakshinamurthi into a Kalyana Sundara (a handsome married man)? It was not just for the destruction of Tarakan and other asuras. Many dead people on earth had to take birth again to elevate themselves and go beyond the cycles of life and death. A supreme, compassionate Ishvara was needed to help them overcome their sorrow and ignorance.'

'As Dakshinamurthi, He had retreated from the world with no thought for this maya-engulfed universe, its inhabitants or their troubles. Ambika (Shakti) became Kameshvari, love incarnate, and made him Kalyana Sundara to change Him from an ocean of knowledge (in the form of Dakshinamurthi) into an ocean of compassion (in the form of Kalyana Sundara). On Her own, She was capable of showering blessings on this world. Though we say She is instrumental in making Him shower blessings on this world, in reality, it is She who does it. To remain unmoving and static is His nature. All actions are Hers. Still, She made it appear that He was the one doing everything. That's all.'

'This is written in the old-style devotional language of the mid-twentieth century by the person who translated it. But see how neatly the guru unpacks this lila for us?'

'He gives Parvati all the credit,' marvelled the mother, who was taking notes, including grown-up words like 'savant' and 'colossus' to explain later to the child as agreed between them.

'Yes, he does. The sacred feminine is not just a pretty doll in our tradition. She's a force, *the* force, who generously gives Shiva credit. But she didn't fool the sage of Kanchi,' smiled the guru. 'I'm not surprised, are you that the would-be temple builders of Delhi went to seek his opinion?'

'Did he help them?' said the child eagerly.

'Oh, yes! He blessed the idea and spread the word. With his backing, this seemingly impossible project suddenly found support across society and in the highest places. Many ordinary people gave what little they could, saying, "Let us pay for at least a brick in the boundary wall of Kumar's temple or a step on the path up to him".'

'The Kanchi seer told the temple committee to find a certain block of granite in the bed of the river Tamraparani in south India. He said that Kumar's main idol should be carved out of that block. How did he know that it was lying there on the river bed, a corner cut off long, long ago to make an image of Shiva? By "chance", they were able to actually locate that very block of stone. An old, bedridden man found by "chance" was able to tell them where he thought it might be. He had heard of it long ago in the village lore of his youth. This man wept with joy when he learnt why they wanted to find that rock in the river. "Now I know why I have stayed alive so long. I can die happily with my duty done," he said through his tears.'

'When the rock was located and brought out, V. Ganapati Stapathi, the master stone carver, checked it out and found that it was perfect according to the rules of the Shilpa Shastra. After he made Kumar's idol, he brought it to the Kanchi seer, who spent the night meditating by it and anointed it with holy ash before it was tenderly taken north to Delhi. The stapathi did such a fine job that he got the National Award the next year.'

'We can divide the sthala puran or founding history of Uttara Swami Malai into four phases. Between 1944 and 1961, the worship of Kartikeya was reintroduced in the north, that too in the country's capital, resulting in the desire to build him a temple in his old homeland.'

'Between 1961 and 1962, with Kartikeya appearing in a dream to a devotee, the desire began to get real with the crucial step of finding and getting the right location which was in harmony with the lost devotional history of Delhi.'

'From 1962 to 1973, with the backing of the sage of Kanchi, the temple took shape stage by stage with the support of the public, of temple trusts across India, and with generous contributions by the government of Tamil Nadu and finally, the support of the Central Government, with the participation of Prime Ministers Lal Bahadur Shastri and Indira Gandhi.'

'The lawyer-politician R. Venkataraman, who became the eighth President of India, was nudged by the sage of Kanchi to take on the role of president of the temple society.'

'This phase of the temple's founding history concluded gloriously in June 1973 with the *kumbhabhishekam* or consecration of the temple by Sri Jayendra Sarasvati, the then-junior Shankaracharya of Kanchipuram. The great Carnatic singer M.S. Subbulakshmi sang for the occasion and no less than the Shivacharya or chief priest of the Madurai Meenakshi temple came to conduct the inaugural puja with due diligence.'

'There's been no looking back since 1973. Kartikeya or "Shivaskanda Murti" as his image is called in Delhi is truly back home and attracts devotees from many regions who enjoy praying to this darling son of Shiva and Parvati. This temple is for anyone who loves them. There's even a Sikh gentleman on the temple management committee.'

'Devotees think that this temple is especially lucky for soldiers and children and for anyone who has problems studying or feels nervous about exams. This is so not only because Kartikeya is a war god but also a symbol of deep learning. Did he not explain the meaning of "Om" to Shiva himself? So Uttara Swami Malai is a strong symbol of our cultural unity across regions in the capital of free India. It's so charming that wild peacocks flock to this temple despite the busy main road below it.'

'I want to see Kumar!' said the child urgently.

'I do, too,' said the father. 'I want to see this poetry-loving warrior god who's come back to us, in the temple that began as the dream of a few young men with no money.'

'We'll all go,' said the grandfather, looking very pleased. 'I've often noticed this temple on the way to the airport. But I had no curiosity about it because I thought it was a south Indian place where I wouldn't know what to do. I had no idea that it was such an organic part of Delhi with a link to the Mahabharata, or that these amazing histories lie hidden in it. I did say that I want us to experience holy places together—and here's one, right under our noses.'

'I want to know more about the sage of Kanchi,' said the grandmother.

The mother, who had quietly Googled for a minute, looked up from her phone. 'Indians in the US are building a *mani mandap* or memorial tower to him in New Jersey!' she exclaimed.

'I'm not surprised. He was "the real thing",' said the guru. 'Anyhow, you'll see the legends of the six chakra temples carved on the outer wall of the main shrine at Malai Mandir. You'll recognize them now, for you know their stories.'

'Oh, and I forgot to tell you something nice. They've added shrines to Ganapati, Parvati and Shiva up there. So say hello to everyone in our First Family, back home together for all to see. How Valmiki, Vyasa and Kalidasa would have liked that.'

8

Kalinath

'While warring factions carry on fighting, the inner life of Bharat, if not India, goes on peacefully,' said the guru after a fortnight. He had gone away to visit friends in the Kangra Valley in Himachal Pradesh and had dropped by after his return, for a cup of tea and a chat with the grandfather. He planned to resume the story sessions on the following Monday.

'What makes you say that, Guruji?' asked the grandfather.

'I saw that for myself last week in Himachal Pradesh, at the seventeenth-century village of Paragpur in Kangra district. So much history has swirled over it, and today it has roads, electricity, schools, clinics, hotels, the internet . . . but despite these lifestyle changes, its habit of faith seems to go on as if nothing has ever happened to it except the lila of the gods. It was very moving,' said the guru.

'Paragpur was apparently the stronghold of the Kuthialas, a branch of the Sood clan, who were treasurers to the royal family of Kangra. Next door to Paragpur is Garli Village, a charming heritage site, which is the old domicile of the Soods, who were Silk Route merchants, builders of cities like Simla, and patrons of commerce and culture. Their old homes show their fascinating cross-continental history—an Italianate villa here, a Chinese lintel there—while not far away the river Beas was apparently witness to the advent of Alexander of Macedonia around 325 BCE. It's all quite amazing.'

'I know what you mean,' said the grandfather. 'Over the last many years I've been by the Beas and on the Beas and across the Beas, and even in the Beas, and there's something about that river. It has so much personality, a mysterious air of "I would if I could" . . . tell stories, I mean.'

'Exactly. When I thought of how much history had flown along with it, and its old rulers, the Katoch clan, who claim descent from the Trigarta kings in the Mahabharata—well, I wanted to nudge the Beas by its shoulder of mauve stone and say in my most cajoling tone, "Vipasha, you most excellent river, won't you tell us of old, forgotten far-off things and battles long ago?"'

'I used to sit by the Beas at sunset to soak in the peace of the deepening twilight. All I could hear was the sound of the river and the call of a night bird or two. Really, what had I expected? That a water sprite would emerge and start telling me fabulous stories, like my grandmother told me in my childhood? I used to walk back irrationally disappointed to the ashram I stayed in. But the Beas gave me a wonderful surprise one morning, something that I could not have imagined despite so many years of being amazed by "the wonder that is India".'

'This happened when I went to visit the temple of Sri Kalinath Kaleshwar Mahadev at Paragpur. Its story goes that in yet another ancient battle between the devas and the asuras, Parvati assumed the fierce form of Kali to defeat the aggressors. But she went on storming even after her victory, out of control . . . and Shiva had had to lie down inert in her path to stop her. Kali stepped right on him, roaring in rage, and only then did she come out of her fury, and recoil in horror when she saw what she had done. She went away then, greatly embarrassed, and it was here, at this site on the banks of the Beas, that Shiva is believed to have brought her out of her depression and made her smile again.'

'It was a story I knew from childhood but I knew nothing of this temple or its connection with this story. Incredibly, the sanyasis of the Niranjana Akhada who attended on "Kalesar" as they call Kaleshwar locally were from south India. They retold the legend in Hindi for me and I came back marvelling at how deep and far the dotted lines run across our country. Wherever you go, you find Mahadev. I felt so blessed that I got to hear the legend of Kalinath Kaleshwar right there by the Beas, where Shiva consoled Parvati and persuaded her to come back home to Kailash.'

'Is it a fine temple?' asked the grandfather.

'The temple itself is simple and relatively new because of the difficult history of the region in the last few centuries before Independence. But the place has an ancient association and a devotional atmosphere. The immense bhakti of the people through all the tides of history has kept its holiness alive to this day. They did not forget their ancient sacred geography. I felt close to Shiva-Parvati there,' said the guru. 'Kalesar gave me back some lost perspective on what is illusion and what is "permanent"—that kings may come and kings may go but God goes on forever.'

'You're quoting again from old English poetry with your own words put in,' teased the grandfather.

'That's right,' laughed the guru. 'Now let me quote directly from the parables of Sri Ramakrishna. This one perfectly illustrates the timeless sense of God that I felt by the Beas.'

Taking out a book from his cloth bag, the guru found the page he wanted and began to read aloud:

'The truth is that God alone is real and all else is unreal. Men, universe, house, children, all these are like the magic of the magician. The magician strikes his wand and says: "Come, delusion! Come, confusion!"

Then he says to the audience, "Open the lid of the pot; see the birds fly into the sky."

But the magician alone is real and his magic unreal.

The unreal exists for a second and then vanishes.

Shiva was seated in Kailash. His companion Nandi was near Him. Suddenly a terrific noise arose.

"Revered sir," said Nandi, "what does that mean?"

Shiva said: "Ravana is born. That is the meaning!"

A few moments later another terrific noise was heard.

"Now what is this noise?" Nandi asked. Shiva said with a smile, "Ravana is dead."

Birth and death are like magic. You see the magic for a second and then it disappears. God alone is real and all else unreal. Water alone is real; its bubbles appear and disappear. They disappear into the very water from which they rise.'

'Ah,' said the grandfather. 'That certainly sums it up.'

'Kalinath Kaleshwar has decided next week's stories for me,' said the guru, getting up to leave.

On his next visit, the guru asked the mother, 'Beti, do you have a map of India?'

'We do, indeed,' said the mother. 'You can see everything on the phone or laptop nowadays but we also like to have a big map to spread out on the table and look at together when we plan holidays.'

She fetched the map and unfolded it on the carpet.

'Look for Unakoti in Tripura,' said the guru to the child.

'Here,' said the child after looking carefully at the north-east.

'Do you know that the ancient goddess of the state is Parvati? She's worshipped as Tripurasundari there in the far north-east—exactly as she is in Tamil Nadu in the farthest south. Unakoti in Tripura is a very special place for Parvati and Shiva,' said the guru.

'Wherever you go, you find Mahadev,' murmured the grandfather.

'You do,' said the guru, smiling at him.

'Even today, in Tripura?' exclaimed the mother. 'So the enemies of religion couldn't kill the gods there, after all.'

'If you mean the Nawab of Bengal in the sixteenth century, he certainly paid the customary friendly visit and broke the old Shiva temples of Tripura,' said the guru. 'But his kingdom, in turn, was swallowed up by the British in 1757 at the Battle of Plassey. Similarly, it was Nadir Shah of Persia who broke the Mughals. Live by the sword, die by the sword. The last Mughals were pensioners of the Marathas. No king stays forever. Only the Paramatma is everlasting!'

'Oh, in my view, it's best to be matter-of-fact about history, that it was the law of the jungle. Meanwhile, here we are together today, as citizens of one republic. It's much better that we all move on positively as friends and fellow-citizens,' said the grandfather.

'But the common people seem to have never given up the grand old gods,' said the grandmother.

'I respect some of the better principles of the Left,' said the guru.

'Really, Teacher?' asked the father.

'Yes, I do. Funnily, they are in tune with some of the things said in the Upanishads and by Acharya Adi Shankara. But I wish the Left had let the gods be. You cannot take away something as interesting as the gods without giving us something better in exchange.'

'People need the gods despite everything . . . or maybe because of everything,' said the grandmother.

'That's exactly it,' said the guru. 'You remember the Shad Ripu, the six enemies released into the world at the time of Creation? They are *kama, krodha, moha, lobha, mada* and *matsarya*—lust, anger, greed, illusion, pride and envy.'

'They exist in each one of us. Thoughts of the gods help us fight these inner enemies. It's a long, tiring battle and we are defeated many times, like Indra was by Vritra. The enemies of religion, being ordinary human beings like everyone else, also had these six inner enemies within them. So, by and by, after throwing out the old kings and the old gods for new, they failed, too, as rulers. As the saying goes, "Power corrupts". And, of course, the old gods came right back into the open after that because they had never really left the hearts of most people.'

'But what happened to Shiva in Tripura?' asked the child, with patient persistence. As the only child and the pet of the family, she was used to being listened to at once. But the storytelling sessions had begun to teach her that some things were a group experience.

'The story goes that Shiva once spent a night in the hills of Unakoti in Tripura on the way back home to Kailash,' said the guru. 'With him were 99,99,999 followers, one short of a crore or "Unakoti". Wanting to get home soon, Shiva asked his followers to wake up well before dawn. However, not one was awake on time except for Lord Shiva himself. So Shiva went off on his own, leaving them behind. When they woke up and realized their mistake, they were too ashamed to move and turned to stone, deciding to stay forever at the place where they had last seen Mahadev. The rocks on the Unakoti hills are said to be the remains of that entourage.'

'Where exactly is Unakoti in Tripura? I would like to see it,' said the grandmother.

The mother read aloud from her phone: 'Unakoti is 178 km to the north from Agartala, the capital of Tripura, and very close to the town of Kailashahar. There are huge rock sculptures at Unakoti, carved from sandstone. The 30 foot high central figure of Shiva has Durga on one side. There's also a gigantic image of Ganapati. Shiva is worshipped as Kal Bhairav at Unakoti and there's a huge fair there every April, called the Ashokashtami Mela.'

'I wonder how old these images are,' said the father.

'Scholars say that they could be from the seventh and ninth centuries. That means almost 1,100–1,300 years ago!' read the mother. 'The legends of Unakoti are found in the *Rajmala*, the chronicles of the Manikya kings of Tripura.'

'*Rajmala* reminds me of *Rajatarangini*, the chronicles of the kings of Kashmir by Kalhana,' said the grandfather. 'I read an English translation long ago. It was done by Ranjit Pandit, the brother-in-law of Pandit Nehru.'

'Any Shiva stories from Kashmir?' asked the mother.

'Best not to go there,' said the father. 'If someone says "Kashmir", all I seem to think of now are our brave soldiers and the wandering dispossessed.'

'I pray for our men and their families, and always, for peace,' said the grandmother, her face clouding.

'I pray, too,' said her son. 'I'm painfully aware of our soldiers constantly fighting terror out there while I get on with my life here.'

There was a sombre pause. 'Kashmir has its own Shaiva Darshan and Abhinavagupta was its most famous scholar a long time ago,' said the guru after a bit. 'The Kashmir Valley was once a nest of Sanskrit singing birds like Kalhana and Bilhana. Acharya went all the way up there to speak to the local scholars. His visit is sanctified on the Shankaracharya Hill in Srinagar. And Parvati has several special temples in Kashmir, especially Kheer Bhavani. The temple's legend links her to the far south. But I can't let you leave the north-east without going to Manipur'.

'Aren't they more Vaishnava than Shaiva in Manipur?' asked the grandmother.

'Yes, they are dedicated to Krishna, but they also dote on Shiva. They know everything there is to know about him, just the same as in the rest of India—that he's one half of God; that he's a dancer and an ashutoshi, easily pleased. And just as others have intimate pet names for Shiva like Bhola or "Innocent" in the north or Koothan the "Dancer" in the south, the Manipuri Vaishnavas consider Mahadev their own.'

'They fondly say, Mahadev is an insane god. That means he's a *bhola*, as innocent as a child. It's a fond way of saying "Pureheart". They understand that side of his personality well. There are famous temples to Mahadev in Manipur at Baruni Hill, Gwarok, Ingurok, Koubru Leikha and Thongam Mondum'.

'How come he's worshipped more as a guru and a dancer in the south and as a *bhola* in the north, west and east?' said the mother.

'Well, he's not Bhola at Kandariya Mahadev temple in Khajuraho in Madhya Pradesh or at Ellora in Maharashtra,' said the father. 'He's Almighty God'.

'Nor is he Bhola at Ujjain, he's "Mahakaal" there. Guruji told us that every Shiva temple of note depicts him on its south wall as the Adi Guru Dakshinamurthi,' said the grandfather.

'Shiva is considered the Adi Guru almost everywhere amongst us,' said the guru. 'It's just that he's so free and happy that he's beyond everything—in a state of such pure bliss that we fondly call him "Bhola" or "childlike" and "innocent". It's not condescending, how can we ever presume to be that with Mahadev, the Great God? No, it's a tribute and an aspiration, both. We don't fully know him or understand him but we sense and want that great joy, that "incredible lightness of being" that Shiva has and also offers us. "*Chidananda rupam Shivoham Shivoham*, I am the joy that's beyond all imagining, I am Shiva." That's how Acharya described him. So it's the same idea across India, be it north, south, east or west. He lives on Kailash and he danced at Chidambaram "and he dances forever in the human heart" as the legend goes. The *Skanda Purana* and the *Brahmanda Purana* spell out our united sacred geography most wonderfully, as do the Sanskrit epics.'

The mother laughed suddenly.

'I just imagined the India of today as a big sponge cake,' she said. 'That sponge cake is Shivbhumi. The big Vaishnava belts like Brijbhumi, Assam, Manipur and Pandharipur are like chocolate marbling in the cake while the big Vaishnava temples dotted around, like Tirupati, Srirangam, Badrinath and others, are like cherries on top. The other religions are like sprinklings of raisins, walnut, pistachio and almond, adding to the taste and texture. And the base, the holding ground for it all, is solidly Shivbhumi, whether it's Durga, Ganapati or Kumar in the forefront or Mahadev himself.'

'Yummy,' said the child. 'Our country is a cake!'

'A delicious thought,' smiled the grandmother.

'It's a fact,' said the guru. 'It's perfectly true'.

'How come it was so easy back in the day to unite the land with the idea of Shiva?' said the father.

'He's the people's god, that's why,' smiled the guru.

'See, Vishnu and Shiva are both aspects of the One. We love them both dearly and most of all, we love the universal mother, the Jagadamba. So this is absolutely not a comparison. It's only a review, if you'd like to call it that, of the separate charms of Shiva and Vishnu, which are one big combined charm, really.'

'Remember what I said about *abhishekha priyo Shiva, alankara priyo Vishnu*? Vishnu is a grand god. He was a king in two avatars. As the Preserver, he's deeply invested in allure and attraction in order to keep creation going. That's his job. Parvati in her role as his "sister energy" helps him as Yogmaya. The path of Vishnu is like a big party. Fine clothes, fabulous jewellery, flowers, lavish decoration, *chhappan bhog* or fifty-six kinds of sweet offerings all at once. It comes with the turf.'

'On Ram Navami, Rama's birthday, every temple in north India throws a free, walk-in lunch for all. The Sikhs join in, as we do at langar in the gurdwara, for we love the heroic Gurus. I can hear the Upanishads in Guru Nanak Dev's verse and I cannot think of Guru Tegh Bahadur without my heart missing a beat. In my view, Guru Gobind Singh was the last true hero in our history, a larger-than-life figure. What a brave, good and learned man! If not constrained by language, I think the whole country would have known about him right then and loved him. He was as proper as Sri Rama himself, with a similar elegance to his nature.'

'Anyhow, all are truly welcome in my neighbourhood temple. No identity cards, no questions. Just walk in, leave your shoes at the door, wash your hands and sit down. Lunch usually starts after the *harati* at noon, the time of Rama's "birth". I use "birth" merely as a term of convenience to describe Mahavishnu's great lila. The Unborn was playing at being "born" for a purpose.'

'But the human pleasure of volunteering to help serve "Rama's birthday lunch" to the poor and to the devout is very real. Those shining steel buckets of pumpkin curry, vegetables in gravy and nourishing halva, those flying trays of fresh, hot puris! The temple committee doesn't skimp for something as special as Rama's birthday lunch. It hires a good, traditional caterer whose team cooks in the big, paved backyard beyond the washbasins, next to the temple garden. A deep, peaceful happiness fills you when you bend to carefully and politely serve the people sitting on lines of mats on the floor of the temple's community hall, rich and poor all together.'

'Shiva has no such feasts. Rather, he has fasts. So he's more complicated and somehow, more simple. Anyone can relate to Shiva, be it a person living in the forest or a suave city person in a fancy villa. The Chenchu tribe, for instance, has important rituals with Shiva in his ancient temple at Srisailam in Andhra Pradesh. It's such an ancient, pre-Buddhist site that the Chinese pilgrims Fa-Hien and Hiuen-Tsang noted it.'

'Though Srisailam is now in Andhra, it's the headquarters (HQ) of the twelfth-century reformist sect of Veerashaivas in Karnataka. Shiva is worshipped as "Mallikarjuna" at Srisailam, as "the Lord, white as jasmine". And north-west of Srisailam, far away on the other side of the country, did you know that the Maharanas of Udaipur, first among equals in Rajputs, ruled their kingdom, Mewar, in Shiva's name?

'Shiva is *that* loved by all, from commoners to kings. How did that happen to a homeless ascetic who also became the father of our First Family, Shiv, Paravati and Ganesh? It can only be because he has some special sort of *saulabhyam* or accessibility, like Vishnu, although he's not an obvious choice. He's not a cute baby, a naughty boy, a ladies' man, a mighty king and a Gitacharya like Sri Krishna, a "someone for everyone" figure. But how we love him!'

'So, what is it, then? Is it the glamour of Parvati that lights up Shiva? Is it those two beautiful children? Is it sturdy, faithful Nandi? No, they're part of his charm but people seem to have loved him just for himself. I can't put my finger on it or label it. It must be personal. Centuries of ecstatic Shaiva poems and plays, from the Himalayas to the Indian Ocean, are proof of it. It's a pure love like nothing else and it's between you and Shiva, it's your own *anubhuti* or experience of sensations and sentiments. It's a mystery, even now.'

'Think about it. He doesn't have straightforward, linear stories with a beginning, middle and end like Vishnu has in the *Ramayana*, *Mahabharata* and the *Srimad Bhagavatam*. Instead, like our religion itself, Shiva has no parents, no beginnings. He always was and is. And he's literally all over the place. He has "incidents", he dances in and out of a whole lot of stories. I'll tell you about his avatars another time, they were whimsical and playful. His devotees were constantly amazed. They were from every section of society and crazy with love for him. What games he played with us foolish mortals!'

'The most beautiful princess in the world, the Mother Goddess herself, chose to marry this homeless, unpredictable ascetic. She was constantly amazed, too, by his doings, "*Girisha charite vismayavati*" as Acharya put it. Yet, girls all over India pray even today for a husband like Shiva, for someone as loyal, loving and respectful. They don't pray for a husband like Rama or Krishna, much as they love and worship the two great princely avatars. However smart and modern the girls are, Shiva is the ideal that goes straight to their hearts. Mahadev is almost quaint, he's that committed to Parvati. But some things don't go out of fashion, I think, in relationships.'

'Shiva's name is the fierce battle cry of soldiers, *Har Har Mahadev*! Yet he's so kind and forgiving to all that even the demons worship him. He has such a special tenderness for the weak that our hearts melt just thinking of it. Orphans see Shiva-Parvati as their father and mother. So you see, he belongs directly to the people, whoever and wherever they are. Even as a guru, he speaks directly to his disciples. Nobody ever needed an intermediary with him. In the old days, if your heart was heavy and you wanted to formally tell Shiva your troubles, all you had to do anywhere in the land was to set up a stone or make a shivling out of mud, offer it water and a bel leaf or a flower and unburden your heart. He always listened and responded, unless there was a reason not to.'

'And all these thoughts could be seen in just a stone?' marvelled the father.

'*Kankar-kankar Shankar samaan*,' said the grandfather instinctively. 'Every stone is like Shiva, meaning it has Shiva in it.'

'True. Such sayings tell us how deep the concept of Shivbhumi goes. Our sacred geography is very particular, like I said, "*Aa Setu Himalaya*" meaning "from the southernmost shores to the northernmost mountains". It was an unknown concept to foreigners. They did not really understand it nor how marrow-deep it goes,' said the guru. 'Let me give you a small but charming instance of "Shiva in every stone". It's from real life, in the far south.'

'A few centuries ago at Chidambaram in what is now Tamil Nadu, there were three families that belonged to a clan of farming landowners, the Veerashaiva Mannadiar. They worshipped Parvati as the goddess Meenakshi, as their *kuladevi* or family deity. A severe drought in and around Chidambaram drove them to migrate to greener lands. One of them took a stone from Chidambaram along with their other things. Worshipping the stone as the representation of Shiva, their friend and guru, they went to several places before reaching Pallasena, a lush green place in Malabar. They settled there and took to trading in diamonds. Whenever they went out on business, they prayed to Shiva by addressing the stone.'

'An old member of their clan was heartbroken that his age and frail health made it impossible for him to travel to see Meenakshi Devi at her temple. He poured out his longing to the stone that the clan had brought from Chidambaram. The old man then proceeded to a pond nearby for his bath. He left his fresh clothes and light palm-leaf umbrella with two boys on the bank. When he came up to the bank from the steps that led into the water, he found that he could not pick up his umbrella. It was rooted to the ground.'

'After a number of people failed to move that flimsy palm umbrella, they called an astrologer, who bathed, said his prayers and went into deep meditation to ask for guidance. He emerged from his trance to say that Meenakshi had made herself present under the umbrella and that was why no one could budge it. Huge crowds thronged to see the miracle. The present Meenakshi temple there and the temple tank next to it were built over the next four centuries. It took so long because of the historical turmoil in the south during those times. The place is called Meenkulati Kaavu or the "abode of the Meenakshi clan" in Palakkad, Kerala.'

'Amazing!' chorused the family.

'It ties up for me with Unakoti, Udaipur, Manipur, Malai Mandir, Pehowa and Paragpur,' said the grandfather. 'Wherever you go, you find Mahadev.'

'So my sponge cake theory is proving right,' said the mother. 'And guess what, I stopped by Wenger's today. Who's for tea, cake and mushroom patties?'

'No cake for me, thank you. You know I'm the boring "eggless" type,' laughed the guru. 'No onions and no garlic either. But I won't say no to a nice cup of tea'.

'No problem, I have mithai and fruit for you, Teacher,' smiled the mother and the child scrambled up from staring wide-eyed at the map of India to go with her.

9

Madurai

'Shiva's relationship with his devotees is unusual, to say the least,' said the guru when they gathered the next week. 'He plays the most childish or bizarre games with them and in turn, he puts up with all kinds of behaviour that no god would tolerate.'

'I'd like to share an extraordinary tale today about such a devotee. It's possible that this story has no parallel in the history of religion. In it, a mere mortal refuses to back down from upholding a fact even when his opponent is God Almighty—and a furious God at that, about to burn him to cinders. "How could he argue with God? What blasphemy!" some would say.'

'Yet this story sits squarely with honour in the mainstream, and its hero is a byword for truth and courage. He is famous for arguing with Mahadev and absolutely refusing to recant. He was a real person, who left his name on a poetic work about Kumar. His legend has never

faded. It was even made into an iconic Tamil movie in the
twentieth century.'

'Let's go back, then, to perhaps the eighth century, to
the kingdom of the Pandyas in the deepest south; and to its
fabled capital, Madurai.'

'Madurai is Tamil for Mathura. Yes, that very Mathura
of the north in Brijbhumi. Mathura is a holy city on the
banks of the river Yamuna. Madurai is a holy city on
the banks of the river Vaigai. Vaigai's Sanskrit name is
Kritamala. She is the younger sister of the Kaveri, who is
also called "Ponni", meaning "the golden one".'

'When the powerful magician, Sage Agastya, came
to the region, he locked up Kaveri in his kamandalu or
sanyasi's waterpot. He did this abominable thing because
he lost his temper when Kaveri got into a big argument
with him about his powers. But Ganapati, the guardian
of the land, did not approve of these strong-arm tactics
that took away a river from its people. He took the form
of a crow, tipped over the kamandalu, flapped his wings in
Agastya's face to say "Who do you think you are?" and flew
away cawing in amusement.'

'The astounded sage could do absolutely nothing
when the river rushed out of the waterpot, laughing, and
dashed away in many directions from where she had been
restrained by Agastya's hand.'

'Kaveri and Agastya made up after this bad start with
Ganapati's diplomatic help, which was a good thing because
Agastya planned to stay in the south and bullying the local
people was not at all the way to win respect or cooperation,
forget affection.'

'To go from the river Kaveri to Madurai on the river Vaigai, was once a beautiful journey across green, fertile land. Madurai was famous those days for its poets and is still famous for the sweetest jasmine in India, the famous "Madurai malli". Do you know that 'malli', which is the common south Indian word for jasmine, is called "malee" in Thailand, Cambodia and Laos and "molee" in China? Words bear witness to who met whom and where. The Tamilians were great seafarers, trading all the way to China.'

'That's a lovely thought. I've heard that a city in South-East Asia is named for Parvati but I don't know which one,' said the mother.

'That's right. It's Phnom Penh, the capital of Cambodia,' said the guru. 'Phnom means "mountain" in Khmer, the Cambodian language. Penh means "girl" or "lady". It's a Tamil word. So "Phnom Penh" means "the Lady of the Mountains". Just as "Malai Mandir" combines a Tamil word and a Hindi word, "Phnom Penh" combines a Khmer word and a Tamil word. And who is that Lady of the Mountains but Parvati of the *parvat*? Her other names like "Girija" and "Haimavati" also mean "Lady of the Mountains", exactly the same as Phnom Penh.'

'Why are we not taught these things in school?' said the father. 'There must be so many interesting things that we don't know about each other.'

'Yes, that has troubled me for years,' said the guru. 'Instead of being taught unifying concepts like *Aa Setu Himalaya* which everyone can share, and the interesting histories of other regions in India, our school books focus mainly on the history of Delhi. This has gone on for decades even after Independence and only serves to divide us and keep us in mutual disregard.'

'The sad fact is that you can't see India from Delhi. All you can see is the Khyber Pass—and Punjab, Rajasthan, Uttar Pradesh and Jammu-Kashmir. It's not a "national narrative" at all but a hugely incomplete story and it only deepens the divide.'

'Why have we done this to ourselves when we are so culturally united underneath in every direction?' said the mother.

'We're culturally united like that by the gods. But are we willing to acknowledge that reality?' said the grandfather.

'The gods have been punished for man's misdeeds, I think . . .' said the grandmother. 'And it's our loss. The gods don't tell us to hate or oppress each other. Men do that.'

'Our society was in decline for centuries because we were neither kind nor united,' said the guru. 'We forgot Shiva in spirit; we kept only to the letter. We became unworthy of divine favour. So whatever happened to us was our own fault. Let us be grown-up and realistic about it. Nobody could have harmed us if we had looked beyond ourselves and been united. Religion was given a new lease each time only because inspiring people were born in age after age. They tried to reform and renew us. Not everyone listened. But to our credit, we have tried hard to reform.'

'My father let me go to school and college only because of Hindu reform,' said the grandmother.

'And I can go to work because of that,' said the mother. 'If so many other people like us had not moved on, I'm not sure what it would have been like.'

'But who was the hero of Madurai who fought with Shiva?' put in the child plaintively.

The grown-ups had a hearty laugh at the timely question, and the guru got on with the story with an apologetic dip of his head at the child.

'It was during the reign of the Pandya king Shenbaga Pandyan that Nakkeeran spectacularly took on Lord Shiva himself and that too in a very civilized way. There was no thumping and yelling, not even one "Ha,ha,ha, ha!" like in religious movies and serials.'

'Nakkeeran was born to a family of conch-cutters. Their craft was dedicated to Parvati, the Supreme Goddess who ruled over Madurai. Her throat was famously praised for being "smooth as a conch", and the people of Madurai, a set of persons addicted to sweet sounds, smells and sights, greatly valued smooth, silky skin in one another.'

'They were a sturdy, clever race, with spears blunted in many territorial battles, and brilliant traders, too, with big, rich markets. The people of Madurai were also spoilt and sensitive because of leading a very good life in their rich, green land nourished by the Vaigai. They constantly celebrated something, as families, as groups of friends and as a city. They took packed lunches wrapped in banana leaves to the riverside for daylong picnics during the festival of Pongal. They watched, heart-in-mouth, as their young men hurled themselves at charging bulls in the sport of "bull-tying" called jallikattu, each prized bull weighing close to half a tonne. They cherished their singers, dancers and poets and celebrated every *vizha* or festival with a flourish of grand processions.'

'Drummers and dancers took the lead in proud Madurai's processions. There were marchers carrying flowered arches, and silken banners on long poles; and tumblers and conjurers and winsome troupes of transgender acrobats and beautiful women whom the whole region came to see as living works of art.'

'The countryfolk drove to town for these processions on bright, jingling carts drawn by sharp-horned cattle. The carpenters, leather-workers, potters, stone-masons and weavers walked proudly past in guilds as did the traders, merchants and soldiers who threw out their chests on parade, and everywhere along the way the people cheered and cheered and flung jasmine buds and golden *champaka* flowers at them celebrating the blissful life of Madurai before they went home to great feasts of spiced mutton, rice, vegetables, fruits and sweets.'

'Madurai was especially famous as the epicentre of Tamil poetry, and Nakkeeran found a place at the Pandiyan court as a poet of eminence. Over time, he became the leader of the Sangam or Literary Academy. Anybody who could compose well had a claim on the court and on the Academy that set the standard for language and literature.'

'Being deeply in love with his queen, King Shenbaga Pandyan decided one day to hold a poetry competition on the eternally pleasing theme of "Woman" with the prize of a thousand gold coins for the winner. The town-crier made the announcement and Madurai began to hum as contenders set to work scribbling on palm-leaves or strode up and down on the banks of the Vaigai hoping for inspiration. Nobody could talk of anything else. The prestige and the prize attached to it awoke the competitive spirit in every poet and would-be poet.'

'In this hubbub, on the day before the poets' assembly, a poor and not particularly bright poet called Dharmi or "Tharumi" in the graceful Madurai accent, wandered into the great temple in which Shiva was worshipped as Kaal Adinath, the Lord of Time.'

'The temple was closed for the afternoon but Tharumi wanted a private word with Mahadev and slipped in quietly. He sat down facing the main inner shrine, his back to a carved granite *thoon* or pillar.'

'"You're a fine one," he told the Great God who lurked at ease behind the shut doors of his shrine, sure of being offered camphor, water, milk, *bilva* leaves and quantities of fruit and flowers several times a day. "You're the Father of the World but you don't seem to care that I'm so poor and hopelessly inadequate as a poet. Nor have I the skill to apply myself to another trade. You know that this city expects everyone to be very good at what they do, particularly poetry, and looks down on untalented people like me. And it's your fault for setting such high standards for Madurai. Did you have to hold the first ever Sangam of antiquity here in my city?"'

'The discouraging silence that followed this rant did not deter Tharumi. "Isn't it time you took a hand in improving my fortune?" he said piteously and stared at Shiva's shrine with equal love and despair.'

'A little cough suddenly sounded behind him and Tharumi looked around in the deep afternoon shade to see who else was there in the temple. He saw an old man standing between the carved granite pillars, holding out a palm leaf.'

'"A verse for you, then," said the old man cordially with the faintest wink, handing it over to the surprised Tharumi. "I'm sure you'll win the king's prize." And as per the norm in these matters, he vanished suddenly. Tharumi ran home, his heart pounding with excitement. He managed to find a clean set of clothes to wear the next day, and ironed them with the heated base of a round brass waterpot.'

'On Poets' Assembly Day, almost all of Madurai was gathered in the big forecourt of the great temple near its *poonkulam* or flower pond, meaning the temple tank. The king sat on a decorated stone platform, surrounded by leading members of the Academy. A spot was marked onstage in front of them for each competitor to come and declaim his verse by turn. All too soon, it was Tharumi's chance, which came at the end. He read aloud from the verse etched on the palm leaf that the mysterious old man had given him and blinked in amazement when roars of applause greeted his recitation, the king applauding the loudest of all.'

'"What wonderful words! The prize must go to you!" said the king graciously while the Academy members nodded in accord.'

'But Nakkeeran got up and said, "No, Your Majesty."'

'"Why not, noble poet?" asked the king.'

'"There is a fault in his verse. He speaks of 'the natural fragrance of a woman's hair', which, as you know, simply does not exist. The fragrance comes from the flowers she wears in her hair, from perfumed hair oil, from the scented soap-nut powder used as a shampoo—or from the smoke of the *sambrani* resin that is burnt on live coals to dry her hair with."'

'"While the Academy grants a due measure of poetic licence in such earth-bound themes, it is not our custom to mislead the public with incorrect information. For instance, in a poem about the *Kurinji* or mountain region, we speak of the flower that blooms naturally there, of the dazzling blue *kurinji* flower that blooms once in twelve years. To serve a rhyme, we do not forcibly transplant the water lily of the *Neydhal* or coast, to the mountains, or the other way around. So I submit that this man's poem does not qualify for the prize—or even as a poem."'

'Tharumi looked wildly at the faces around him that had beamed in approval a moment ago and were now curling with scorn.'

'"This is not my poem!" he stuttered. "Please wait, I'll fetch the man who gave it to me", and bolted from the stage before anyone could stop him. The king shrugged and the scholars of the Academy began to review the other poems that they had shortlisted.'

'Meanwhile Tharumi ran into the Shiva temple and began to pound on the pillars with his fists, wailing to Mahadev to rescue him from certain death. The old man obligingly appeared on cue and led the way back to the assembly, telling Tharumi to calm down.'

'Striding up to the platform, the old man, with Tharumi stumbling behind, made his way boldly to the king, bowed low and coolly asked what the problem was.'

'Nakkeeran, at a nod from King Shenbaga Pandyan, repeated his objection.'

'"Very well," said the old man smoothly. "Perhaps not in the case of an ordinary woman. But surely the queen of our fair land may be said to have a natural fragrance to her hair?"'

'The crowd gasped at the impertinence while the king frowned and regretted that he had chosen such a double-edged sword of a theme.'

'"Now let the old curmudgeon get out of *that*," thought Nakkeeran's jealous rivals in the Academy, almost purring aloud in malice.'

'But, "No", said Nakkeeran with icy politeness. "I'm afraid not. Our noble queen, though the queen, is nevertheless a mortal woman."'

'"What about the celestial maidens then, the *apsaras*?" said the old man, smiling faintly in appreciation of this irrefutable snub.'

'"We have no means of verifying that possibility," said Nakkeeran, annoyingly to the point again. The king laughed suddenly and so did a few members of the Academy while the crowd chuckled openly at this comprehensive put-down.'

'Tharumi stole a look at the old man and suddenly cried out in fear.'

'The old man stood very straight and tall now and his limbs shone with unearthly lustre. He looked furious and a terrifying vertical crease glowed fiery red in the middle of his forehead.'

'"The Lord God!" whimpered Tharumi and fell to his knees.'

'"Shiva-Shiva!" exclaimed the king, his courtiers and the citizens in shock and awe and sank to their knees, too.'

'Only Nakkeeran was left standing and bowed composedly to the old man who bore the unmistakable sign of being Lord Shiva himself.'

'"Tell me, Nakkeeran," said the old man sternly into the silence with a look at cowed, kneeling Madurai, "you worship Parvati, don't you, as Poon Kodai, the goddess with flowers in her hair, in this very city? And you worship Shiva, as Kaal Adinath the Lord of Time. They are your personal deities. You dedicate your words and deeds to them every single day. Would you go so far as to say that even Parvati has no natural fragrance to her hair?"'

'Nakkeeran stood very still, thinking fast. Shiva was clearly playing one of his mystifying games and he, Nakkeeran, must find his lines and play along, risking all.'

'Drawing a breath, Nakkeeran looked his beloved god straight in the eye. Politely, firmly and slowly, he said, "Even if it's the Lord with the eye in his forehead, a fault is a fault".'

'Nakkeeran had very properly refused to be drawn into an unseemly debate about the Goddess, in whose praise no words and no flights of worshipful fancy were good enough, and thrown the ball right back at Shiva. The crowd sighed to hear him and closed its eyes, unable to look.'

'It's said that Nakkeeran then took a flying leap into the temple tank to escape the blaze from Shiva's third eye, that annihilating look that had incinerated Kama, the god of love; that fiery blaze from which Kumar, the War Lord, was born.'

'But he came to no harm for Shiva liked it very much that Nakkeeran, though a puny mortal, had stood up to him with such polite conviction. Nakkeeran had even indirectly scolded Shiva for having brought Parvati's name into the argument. He had stopped the matter right there by refusing to take Parvati's name and firmly saying, "A fault is a fault" to Shiva himself.'

'As a matter of fact, Shiva went away greatly pleased by this lila that a lesson had been imparted to the public to think things through, to respond appropriately and not take even God's word for it.'

'The king gave the bag of gold to Nakkeeran for his immense courage and for having enabled them all to get a glimpse of the Great God.'

'In thanksgiving to Mahadev for having spared him, Nakkeeran begged the king to spare Tharumi and gave half the gold to the lying poet although it was not his poem at all and remained as faulty as ever.'

10

Nagchampa

'I'm reading a very interesting book on the sacred trees and plants of India,' said the guru on his next visit, which was 'unofficial'. He had taken to dropping by regularly for a cup of tea and a cosy chat with the grandfather. Their bond went back a good forty years and the family story sessions were making it stronger.

'And we couldn't stop talking about Nakkeeran,' said the grandfather. 'We've all been fantasizing about what we'd do if Shiva suddenly stood before us. I said that my heart would burst or I'd fall down in joy. But I don't think I could say a word.'

'Mahadev is capable of anything,' said the guru. 'He's a master actor, a *baazigar*. Knowing that he likes to dress up and play-act in our midst, I take good care to be polite to every single person I meet. What if it's Mahadev in disguise? It may sound silly but I actually think that. I suppose he is my inner moral compass. Of course, we should be polite to everybody anyway. But it's easier somehow to play along with the notion of the lila. It's more fun that way, and it pleases me to think that people I meet or pass by could be Mahadev himself, on his way to doing something extraordinary.'

'I like the idea very much. The child will love it,' said the grandfather.

'Our story sessions have made me realize just how much the concept of sacred geography has been thought through to the last detail,' said the guru. 'For instance, this book on our sacred trees and plants by two Indian authors is a real eye-opener. We know of course that durba grass, tulsi, parijat, pipal and bel are holy. Not only are trees in general considered "Brahma's hair" but also, as I may have told you, every temple has a particular tree, its own *sthala vriksha*. But I didn't know much about sacred trees like the kadamba and the nagchampa or flowers like the golden champaka, except where they're listed in the epics.'

'Do tell me more,' said the grandfather.

'Take the kadamba. I've grown up knowing that Radha and Krishna are supposed to have met in its sweet shade. It appears a lot in the *Srimad Bhagavatam*. But I didn't know for a long time that while the north associates it with Krishna, in the south it is categorically known as the "Parvati Tree". Parvati is described in some Sanskrit verses as "*Kadamba-vana nilaye*" and "*Kadamba-vana vasini*", the "Dweller of the Kadamba Forest". The kadamba's trade name in the lumber business is in fact the Parvati Tree.'

'The epics, I realize, never stop naming and celebrating trees and flowers. For instance, in the Valmiki Ramayana 3:15, which is the Aranya Kandam, Sarga fifteen, we get to see the making of a very special woodland home. The Three have arrived in the flowering forest of Panchavati in a green valley by the Godavari with mountains around it.'

'They're looking for a place in which to build their little cottage, as safe as possible from the snakes and wild animals. Rama notes the ideal location of a forest glade full of flowering creepers and shrubs. It is conveniently by the banks of the Goda on which they see swans and chakravaka birds swimming about just as Rishi Agastya told them they would.'

'The coppery mineral streaks in the mountains catch the light and gleam like the oval vents in the houses and buildings left behind at home in Ayodhya or like the painted hides of the elephants in the Ikshvaku stables. There's a lake near the glade in which deep pink and pure white lotuses bloom. Thick kusa grass grows handily around for the daily personal prayers.'

'Sita, who loves gardens and parks, finds the air sweet with the scent of golden champaka flowers. Rama is delighted to see many kinds of trees—sal, tamal, jackfruit, mango, date-palm, ashok, shami and kimshuk. He turns to strong, sturdy Lakshmana and says, "Will you make a parnashala for us, a thatched cottage in this pleasant place by the Godavari?"'

'He doesn't give Lakshmana a single order nor does Sita tell him "Do this! Do that!" In fact, the fond joke in religious discourses is that being a princess, Sita didn't know the a-b-c of housekeeping and was even happier than Rama that Lakshmana came with them to cook dinner and do the dishes.'

'Of course, there are also those who accusingly ask, "And what about Urmila?" *Arre bhai*, how do we know what she really thought of it all? What we do know is that Lakshmana was a short-tempered fellow, ready to fight everybody at once. Rama had to keep telling him not to flare up and to please calm down. For all we know, Urmila was quite happy to stay back comfortably in the palace at Ayodhya and have a nice, long holiday from having to manage Lakshmana. She may have handed him over to Rama gladly enough, saying, "Please take charge of him". If Valmiki does not elaborate on it, it shouldn't worry us unduly. Maybe he was being discreetly silent, you know. But so many people want to poke about accusingly. It's a compliment to Valmiki I suppose that everyone wants to be cleverer than he or catch him out in some way.'

'The epics are irresistible like that. We tell and retell them, tell and retell them, and try to split one hair into seventy-six. It's what we've done for millennia and their savour shows no sign of fading. Look at us, for instance, what a task we've begun, trying to gather interesting bits and pieces about Shiva, who is intertwined inextricably with Parvati, Vishnu, Ganapati, Kartikeya and his devotees, the whole pack of them. That Shiva who is infinite, without beginning and end! Are we likely to know or tell "everything"? Of course we can't. We'll never be done, for the topic is much bigger than us all.'

'To get back to Project Parnashala, old-style commentators like to remind us here that because Lakshmana is the avatar of Adisesha, the cosmic serpent, he's bound to serve Vishnu anyway in his avatar as Rama.'

'But story-wise, in their earthly situation, it's such a nice, modern gesture of trust and delicacy that Rama and Sita quietly leave the task to Lakshmana, who has never made a cottage before. It's the kind of thing that Shiva and Parvati might do if they took an avatar.'

'Lakshmana gets to work, raising a high clay floor, making strong pillars of bamboo for the clay walls, with rafters of shami branches and a snug thatch of "kusa" and "kaasa", grass and leaves.'

'He has independent charge of the project and makes an admirable cottage which is so tactfully and appropriately built that it thrills Rama and Sita. Rama is so moved that he hugs Lakshmana and says, "It's like Father is back". He means that Lakshmana has shown so much love and care in making the parnashala that Rama, grieving for Raja Dasharatha, feels comforted.'

'As family situations go, it seems to be about giving each other space and doing our thoughtful best for each other. Valmiki is subtle in this. He creates touching incidents and vivid scenes in which we may appreciate the nuances ourselves.'

'How beautiful this country must have been once! How did it get so dirty and depressing when we had such idyllic landscapes?' said the grandfather.

'Wait till you see Bali. It is heartbreakingly like what India could have looked like without the dirt and disorder.'

'I liked hearing about the cottage in Panchavati,' said the grandfather. 'It's interesting how epic references turn up everywhere in real life. When I took my son to Ujjain, I told him we were going to the place where Krishna had gone to boarding school, at Rishi Sandipani's gurukul. My son immediately remembered the story of Krishna and Sudama; and Sudama's famous gift of poha to Krishna when he went to see him at Dwaraka. We were so surprised and pleased to find that poha is the most popular local snack in Ujjain. It was such a charming epic link.'

'There's a very nice Haryanvi song about Krishna and Sudama in which Krishna fondly reproaches Sudama for not coming to him sooner. It's the most touching song I've heard in a long time,' said the guru. 'A schoolgirl from Haryana, a farmer's daughter, made it very popular. I'm told that more than one crore people know this song.'

'Do play it,' said the grandfather, and the guru took out his phone and found the song on YouTube. They sat back to hear the sweet, hypnotic strains of *Bataa mere yaar Sudama re (Tell me dear Sudama)*.

'The child will love this,' said the grandfather, 'they all will. *Kyun bhullya pyaar Sudama re*—why did you forget my love, Sudama? That takes me to the heart of our faith.'

'Moving, isn't it? To think of Sri Krishna and Sudama in Dwaraka, and in gurukul out in the green Malwa Plateau. I like the Indian heartland for many reasons. On my visit to Ujjain, I found the roads and general cleanliness quite good except for a messy section at Ramghat on the holy river Kshipra, which had the usual detritus of plastic bags, dead flowers and mud. But the walls along the roads of Ujjain were beautifully painted with decorative motifs in terracotta on white. The charm of a small town with little traffic and many trees and parks instantly made me wistful for the "quality of life" that has gone missing from our now-toxic mahanagaris'.

'Not surprisingly, the local Hindi is very good, too,' said the grandfather. 'I noticed that the menu-board of even a small roadside dhaba said '*Do Nug*' in chaste Hindi for "two pieces" per plate of paranthas or toasted cheese sandwich, whereas a "jumbletown" like Dilli says "*Do Piece*" even when written in Devnagari.'

'I liked the graceful, old-fashioned manners on the street,' said the guru. 'There is definitely a soft charm to the place. All you have to do is say "Namaste" to get smiles and help. In that sense, Madhya Pradesh is like the rest of India. The key to it is old-fashioned politeness—a Please, a Thank You and a smile along with a Namaste. Everybody knows exactly how to behave then and it can be very pleasant and civilized.'

'How was your experience at the Mahakaleshwar temple?' asked the grandfather.

'Mixed,' said the guru. 'I went there in winter. I could walk in, warmly clad in jeans, right into the sanctum and nobody objected. Women in jeans walked in, too, without any trouble. I thought the bare-chested priests, hardened by the rigour of service, looked elegant in their red, yellow, *gerua* or purple cotton dhotis.'

'The general arrangements were very nice and the staff and security personnel were very polite, especially at the lockers and the footwear counter. The Ramakrishna Mission has a nice little bookshop in the inner compound. I noticed that it also had books on Christianity and Islam comfortably displayed next to books on Hinduism.'

'But right inside the sanctum, the way some men in uniform, and pilgrims from elsewhere in India, pushed and shoved in the queue was not nice at all. What an irony, really! Imagine pushing and shoving and making haste at any temple, that too at a temple that specifically celebrates Shiva as Eternity. Anyhow, thanks to CCTV, I could see the *harati* all the way along the queue. There was absolutely no need to hurry. Ultimately, it was watching the quiet sincerity of many other devotees that gave me a sense of *darshan*.'

'Yes, I can understand that. You mentioned the nagchampa earlier. That sounds like it could be either Shaiva or Vaishnava,' said the grandfather.

'Ah,' said the guru, beaming. 'Do you know what a great point you just made? It seems that every epithet of Shiva is interchangeable with every epithet of Vishnu, if you dig deep into the meaning. All but one. The name Narayana that we find most famously in Vishnu's *ashtakshari* or eight-syllable mahamantra—*Om Namo Narayanaya*. And that, if you please, is exclusive to him not because of theology but because of a rule in Sanskrit grammar.'

'Really? I never thought of Vaakvani Sarasvati as a . . . what do you call it? A grammar-nazi!' laughed the grandfather.

'Oh, she's very strict,' said the guru. 'Now you've reminded me of the late Frits Staal.'

'The Sanskritist?' said the grandfather.

'Yes, Frits Staal, the Dutch scholar. I have a clipping on him that I would like to read to you because it's about *devbhasha* Sanskrit,' said the guru, reaching out for his trusty cloth bag.

Putting on his glasses, he began to read:

'Frits Staal, 1930–2012, was Emeritus Professor of Philosophy and South/South-East Asian Studies at the University of California. He studied at Amsterdam and Varanasi, and obtained his PhD from the University of Madras as a government of India scholar . . .'

'And so Frits went to Madras in 1954, walking daily under a large black umbrella to learn Sanskrit from a pandit who taught little children. He discovered that "Sanskrit was much more alive in India than Classical Greek and even Latin in Europe".'

'Importantly, Frits met and was influenced by Professor V. Raghavan, member of the government of India Sanskrit Commission, consisting of the eight most renowned Sanskrit scholars of India. Their report recommended the three-language formula and the creation of the Central Institute of Indology.'

'Frits said that he found Raghavan's outlook "truly universal", supporting not only Sanskrit but all classical languages. Quoting from an article he wrote in remembrance. "What I learned from Raghavan was that Panini and the classical languages paved the way for the artificial languages of modern science, for classical languages concentrate on the transmission of knowledge. Raghavan showed that there is no limit to the interplay between traditions and innovations within a civilization."'

'In 1975, Frits organized the twelve-day Vedic sacrifice Atiraatra-Agnicayana with the learned priests Cherumukku Vaidikan and Itti Ravi Nambudiri in Kerala. He was supported by prestigious foreign funders. Two monumental documentary volumes on *Agni* emerged as a result in 1983.'

'Fascinating,' said the grandfather. 'It makes me want to hear the Sri Rudram again on YouTube. This is my favourite verse:

"*namaste astu bhagavan*
vishveshvaraya mahadevaya tryambakaya
tripurantakaya trikagni-kalaya kalagni rudraya
nilakanthaya mrutyumjayaya sarveshvaraya
sadashivaya shriman mahadevaya namah"

O Lord, we salute You.
Lord of the Universe, the greatest of all,
With the three all-seeing, all-knowing eyes
Who confers on us the ultimate knowledge and
    enlightenment,
O Lord, who devours past, present and future like fire
    within himself.
Blue-necked one, conqueror of death, Lord God of all,
The Cause of everything, Great God, we salute You.

'It makes my hair stand on end,' said the guru.

'But . . .' said the grandfather, looking embarrassed, 'I no longer know what to think of some scholars. I absolutely don't condone virulence and violence against them. I feel smirched by that. Smirched! However, I also have to admit that some interpretations get on my nerves.'

'Nobody knows what to think any more, so you're not alone,' said the guru, holding out an old issue of *Biblio* magazine. 'But look, we can cheer up with the nagchampa. Would you like to read aloud the part I've marked? It's from an article about the book I'm reading on our sacred plants.'

The grandfather took the magazine and began to read aloud:

"'. . . the punnaga or nagchampa (Alexandrian laurel/ *Calophyllum inophyllum L.*), which is neither 'Alexandrian' nor 'laurel', a fact drily noted by the authors, is a hard wood best known today for prosaic uses like making railway sleepers and cabinets."

"It yields dark, viscous oil that smells and tastes unpleasant and is moreover poisonous. Its oil is used in making soap. But this stolid-sounding tree is otherwise crimson-leaved and makes a good shade tree for avenues."

"Not nearly exciting enough? Wait, the punnaga is discovered to carry the salt tang of the wide oceans, the romance of the ancient seafaring race of the Tamils from the heady days of the Pallava kingdom and the Chola Empire. It was punnaga wood that was used to build their ships for trade, and once, a blue water navy for the conquest of a king of Sumatra who harassed Indian traders. The Indian force made its point and sailed back home, it did not loot or colonise the kingdom."

"This stout tree, besides carrying adventurous Indians over the waves, is also discovered to protect the shoreline along the Eastern Seaboard. It is under its wide and hospitable shade that the Parava fisherfolk ritually picnic on rice and fish curry and pray to its tree spirit for a good catch."

"These interesting affiliations to everyday life add to the lustre of the punnaga and we may read on to learn that the punnaga finds frequent mention in Valmiki's *Srimad Ramayanam*, appearing in the Bala Kandam, in Kubera's pleasure garden 'Chaitraratha', in the Kishkinda Kandam, and most poignantly as one of the decorative trees around the pretty cottage in Panchavati forest, the scene of Sita's dreadful abduction."

"The punnaga is often to be found in the *Mahabharata* as well, notably as witness to Nala's abandonment of Damayanti in the forest, and looking on at the sacred lake of Dvaitavana where Duryodhana comes to taunt the Pandavas in exile on the excuse of inspecting his herds and branding cattle."

"After these epic revelations, it is a pleasant drift through mythological time to the *Matsya Purana*, *Vishnu Purana* and to the holy of holies, the *Srimad Bhagvatam*, the biography of Sri Krishna, where the Purana says that the punnaga may be found on Trikuta Mountain, in SB 8:2.9-13."

"Tamil literature and Chola inscriptions further attest to the special position enjoyed by the punnaga."

"But we hit gold, as it were, when we come to an enduring Chennai landmark, the Kapalisvarar temple at Mylapore, for at this ancient landmark, the punnaga was and is the tree of trees."

"In the Shiva-Parvati lore of the Kapalisvarar temple, it is under a punnaga that Parvati undertook her worship of Shiva and was reunited with him after a separation. Similarly, the punnaga is central to the sacred legends of the Shaiva temples at Thanjavur, and at Tuticorin, famed for its pearl-fishers."

"Beguiled by these marvels, it is almost with affection that we finally discover that among its medicinal uses, the punnaga—always the punnaga now, or if you will, the nagchampa, but never the Alexandrian laurel—that is to say, the punnaga will also cure ulcers, relieve muscle and joint pain and even treat nervous disorders: in all, a most excellent tree to become acquainted with."

"So it goes, through the rest of the book, with some entries shorter and some much longer. Particularly recommended are the entries on the Tamarind, the Plantain and the Sal. The entry on the famous Soma of the Vedas contains the intriguing fact that 'bhang' is an epithet of Soma in the Rig Veda, so perhaps it was, after all, hemp or *Cannabis sativa*—'a medicinal shrub grown on the foothills of the Himalayas and in Pakistan. This seems the most likely explanation for Soma' note the authors. This entry is one of the most impressively researched and articulated.'"

'Did you enjoy that?' said the guru anxiously, in case his friend was tired.

'Yes, I did, thank you. It's a clear case of "Wherever you go, you find Mahadev". And imagine Indian ships made of nagchampa wood sailing over the seas all the way to China via Sumatra. Also, the riddle of Soma is practically solved, I see. It could be what we always thought it was—Mahadev's special drink, bhang.'

'There's a sting in the tail, though,' said the guru, his dark grey eyes alight with amusement. 'Read the last part, will you, after Soma?'

'Oh?' said his friend and took up the article:

"'As to which the authors, as Indian researchers of experience, 'own' this cultural knowledge. Only its botanical formatting is of fairly recent Western origin. Therefore they may like to boldly replace inappropriate colonial labels like 'Wooden Beggar Bead' for the holy Rudraksha (*Eleocarpus sphericus*) in future editions and reconsider the need to reflexively cite a Western writer—'Stutley 1985, 119'—for information like 'The five divisions of the berry signify Shiva's five faces'. The Western researcher would have obtained such information from an Indian in the first place. As Indian experts themselves, they do not need citations for such cultural basics.'"

'And . . . ?' said the guru, an eyebrow raised.

'You're a wicked person, Guruji,' chuckled the grandfather. 'I never noticed all these years. I had you labelled as mild and saintly. But speaking of Shiva is proving most instructive.'

11

Ganga

'We say *Hari bhakti* but *Shiva jnana*,' said the guru at the next story session. 'That means "devotion to Vishnu and knowledge of Shiva". This is not a narrow, literal definition. It's a deep summary of their combined essence. We need them both on our personal journey through our human birth. Especially, we need the grace of Devi. I need a separate katha series for her, there's so much to try and say. Our religion generously allows us to choose the aspect of God that we like most for our personal focus. But both Vishnu as the Gitacharya Krishna and Shiva as Adi Guru Dakshinamurthi tell us that life is a short, passing drama. The only path through it is love.'

'When we define that love as "God love", it does not mean love only for the image of God in a temple or in our puja corner. God is present in everything and everybody. So the message is, "Be loving to everybody". How can we do that? For one, never initiate a quarrel or a cruelty. By all means defend yourself if someone attacks you. But let the matter be after that; don't carry a grudge forever. Above all, give of yourself. Give in service, give in charity, give in affection and give with good manners. My grandmother used to say, "*Kuch bhi bolo par meetha bolo*". Say anything you please, but say it "sweetly", meaning politely, and in a nice tone. This is not "weakness", it's manners.'

'Manners, manners, manners! Manners at home, manners on the street, manners at work. Phone manners, lift manners, road manners. Not overtaking from the left, not honking loudly and needlessly. Not driving fast in the wrong place, not endangering others or making them uncomfortable, not being intrusive—all these things are manners, and each time we show good manners and soft speech, our behaviour is like an offering to God. This is *dhyana* or meditation in real life. This *dhyana* leads us to *jnana*.'

'Use a nice, egoless tone with the garbage collector who comes to your door. Use it with shop assistants, plumbers, carpenters, electricians, fruit and vegetable sellers, with everyone who provides you a service. Use it with elders, visitors and strangers. Use it lavishly at home and work. It softens everybody's day. The good energy that they will get and automatically pass on from you will lift up the whole atmosphere and come back to you.'

'Especially, when you give to beggars, hold your hands below theirs. Let their hands be above yours. Let them take your money from above, not receive it from below. This small but important change in your body language is noted by God because it means that you are showing love. Sri Krishna says in the Bhagavad Gita, in Canto nine Verse twenty-six:

"patram pushpam phalam toyam
yo me bhaktya prayacchati
tad aham bhakti–upahrtam
asnami prayatatmanah"

'"Just a leaf, a flower, a fruit or some water is enough for me. I accept it. But what I want is your love; what you offer is the vehicle that carries your love to me." If we "offer" rather than "give" to the needy, it's as though we're making an offering to God. It is *Hari bhakti*.'

'Sri Krishna himself takes us to Shiva in the *Bhagavad Gita*. He says, in Canto four Verse thirty-seven:

"yathaidhamsi samiddho 'gnir
bhasma-sat kurute 'rjuna
jnanagnih sarva-karmani
bhasma-sat kurute tatha"

'"As the blazing fire turns firewood to ashes, Arjuna, so does the fire of knowledge burn to ashes all reactions to material activities."'

'To know and understand that life is short and not worth negative behaviour and to practise soft speech and behaviour instead is *Shiva jnana*. Shiva is the fountainhead of knowledge. When all is gone, only the ultimate essence is left—the *moola tattvam*—which is water. The world itself is mostly made of water. Our bodies, too, are mostly made of water.'

'We literally put earth and water on our bodies with *vibhuti* and *chandan* to remind us of this truth.'

'There is another kind of holy water that we drink, not through our mouth but through our ears. This sweet water for our souls is made of ragas. Ragas are a holy gift, for it was Shiva who invented speech, music, dance and philosophy and made Sarasvati their custodian. He created everything with the first syllable "Om". Let me tell you about one very special raga, called Shankarabharanam.'

'"Shankar-Abharanam" means the "Ornament of Shiva". The *Brahmanda Purana* tells an old tale called the "Bhadragiri Mahatmyam", of how Narada, the wandering sage, once stopped by that place. He found a temple there to Shiva as "Chandrachudesvara", the "Moon-bearer". So Narada sat down and played sweet music on Mahathe, his divine veena, as an offering to Shiva.'

'Suddenly, an iridescent green iguana or giant lizard flashed by. Narada could tell with just that one glimpse that it was Mahadev who had teased him in that disguise. But he could make no sense of it. Baffled, Narada went off to Satyaloka, the abode of Brahma, to beg for an explanation.'

'Brahma laughed and informed Narada that he had been rewarded with a glimpse of a lila between Shiva and Parvati.'

'"Which lila was that?" said Narada.'

'"Shiva happened to visit Bhadragiri one day. It was so green and pleasant that he wanted to lure Parvati there. He took the form of a jewel-like iguana and frisked about in the sunshine. Parvati spotted the dancing gleam from faraway Kailash and went to investigate. She was charmed to see the beautiful iguana."'

"'Chasing the entrancing creature, Parvati managed to touch the tip of its green tail. At once, she found her own body gleaming with an emerald hue. That is how she got the name 'Maragathavalli', meaning 'the green-hued-goddess'. The name commemorates this particular lila. It was played by Shiva because he liked Bhadragiri and wanted to bless it that it should stay evergreen. So he got Parvati to come there and play with him. This game was their blessing on Bhadragiri.'"

"'Bhadragiri was indeed very beautiful,' said Narada. "That is why I was inspired to sit down and play my veena for Shiva when I found a temple to him there as Chandrachudesvara.'"

"'You must have pleased him very much, which is why he rewarded you with a look at his lila,' said Brahma. "Which raga did you play?'"

"'Shankarabharanam,' said Narada.'

"'No wonder he was pleased,' said Brahma. "You know that Mahadev is also Vaidishvar, the god of healers. Shankarabharanam is a healing raga. The power of this raga to cure emotional disturbance and pain is beyond words. Many people on earth say that they feel lifted to great heights of devotion after listening to Shankarabharanam. They claim that they feel fearless and empowered, as if they can sense Shiva's hand on their head.'"

"'Thank you for shedding this light on my mysterious experience,' said Narada and wandered off, delighted to have pleased Mahadev . . .'

'Can we hear this raga nowadays?' said the grandmother.

'Oh yes, most certainly. It resembles Raag Bilaval in Hindustani music. "Bilaval" is said to have come from "Velavulli", a tribe that migrated from the plains of the north to the hills of the south. Just look on YouTube for it,' said the guru. 'You can hear this raga as both Shankarabharanam and Bilaval. They're both out there for all to hear. They're the same thing, just expressed differently—"unity in diversity".'

'I like Bilaval very much,' said the mother, the singer, eyes sparkling, 'I want to share this story with my colleagues'. But then, her face fell. 'Not everyone likes classical music. Some people find it boring. And me with it,' she said.

'Classical music is a cultivated taste,' said the guru soothingly. 'You should not feel defensive because you like it. We are free to like everything—classical music, film music, folk music, world music. Ragas run through almost everything. As you know, film music has a lot of ragas in it and some outstanding songs. My own favourite is Raag Kedar. There are wonderful old film songs set in it. And I love *Kanha re Nandanandan* in Kedar by Ustad Rashid Khan.'

'So which song in Bilaval or Shankarabharanam should I share with my colleagues?' said the mother.

'If you want a spiritual song, I like *Rab so neha lagao re manva*, "Make friends with God, my mind and heart". It's a variation sung by Pandit Ajoy Chakraborty and his daughter Kaushiki. If you want a film song, there's a national favourite in Bilaval that I think everyone must have heard—*Dil hai chhota sa* from *Roja*. You listen a bit and choose the one that you think they would like,' said the guru. His eyes shone with a sudden glint of fun. 'Mind you, there's another song, just a note away from "pure" Shankarabharanam. I think almost everyone would like that, too.'

'Now which song is that?' said the grandfather, leaning forward. He had watched the guru's face closely and spotted the gleam in his eye.

'It begins with the words *"Jana gana mana"*,' said the guru and put his tongue firmly in his cheek.

A burst of appreciative laughter greeted this disclosure.

'Unbelievable!' said the father. 'God works in mysterious ways.'

'It's almost spooky,' laughed the mother. 'The gods pop up just everywhere in our lives.'

'Like in "Name, Place, Animal, Thing"?' said the child.

'Yes,' said the mother, 'In everything.'

'Every stone,' smiled the father.

'Every tree and plant,' said the grandfather, looking at the guru.

'Wait, there's more. The national anthem of Pakistan is also set in Shankarabharanam, that is to say, in Raag Bilaval,' said the guru. 'You know that Bangladesh and India share a poet in their national anthems—Rabindranath Tagore wrote both songs. Meanwhile, you could say that Pakistan and India share a raga in their national anthems.'

'Good Lord!' said the father.

'Yes, *Pak Sarzameen* is musically akin to *Jana Gana Mana*. It must be one of the least noticed things in the world since the media only reports how this group or that in India quarrels about our anthem,' said the guru.

'This goes deep, like Malai Mandir—an old pattern in the soil of the subcontinent that asserts itself,' said the father.

'Yes, it's bigger than all of us. It's an earth song that won't be silenced.'

'Wherever you go, you find Mahadev,' murmured the grandfather to himself.

'I love the thought that we mark ourselves with earth and water by applying *vibhuti* and *chandan*,' said the grandmother. 'Won't you talk to us about the Ganga, Teacher? We all know the story of how Bhagirath got the Ganga to come down to earth. We know about Mahadev taking the force of her fall on his own head. We know that she flows from the Himalayas to the Bay of Bengal. We know about the important towns on her banks. But there's so much we don't know about her, considering that so many people in the furthest corners of our country keep Ganga water in their homes and temples.'

'The Ganga is definitely a "she", unlike her mighty brother to the north-east, the Brahmaputra,' said the guru. 'You can find the hand of sacred geography in the waters, too. First of all, take the Arabian Sea to the west and the Bay of Bengal to the east. These are recent names. The old Indian names for these two great seas are beautiful— "Ratnakara" for the western sea and "Mahodadhi" for the eastern sea.'

'Now take the rivers. Most Indian rivers flow eastwards. They are called "nadi". A few rivers flow west like the Sharavati in Karnataka of Jog Falls fame, the Narmada and the Tapti. Technically, they should be called "nada", not "nadi". However, since most of our rivers flow east, the common word for river is "nadi".'

'By the way, it's not a long "aa" at the end of "nada". It's "uh", the way I said it, "naduh". It's the same for Shiva, Rama, Krishna, Lakshmana and so on. Shivuh, Ramuh, Krishnuh, Lakshmanuh. But spelling it like that in English would create more confusion and take us even further away. Meanwhile what happened is that the north cut off the "uh" at the end and simply says "Ram" while the south stretched that 'uh' into "aa" and says "Raamaa". These regional styles are here to stay. But it's interesting how we all automatically switch to "uh", north, south, east and west, when we pray in Sanskrit.'

'I'll give you an example that I like very much; it's something that I say every day. Here's how it came to be. In the *Mahabharata*, Bhishma, lying on his bed of arrows, answers Yudhishtira's six questions to him about God—who is "God", whom should we worship, and so on. Bhishma answers with the *Vishnu Sahasra Namam*, the thousand names of Vishnu. Vishnu has many thousands of names but this particular set from Bhishma contains the names given by the ancient rishis. Names like "*Vishvam Vishnur-Vashatkaro . . .*'

'Up on Kailash, Shiva and Parvati hear Bhishma's recitation. Parvati, the universal Mother, immediately wants to share it with her children on earth. For our sake, she asks Shiva how this long prayer may be recited easily by all. That's when Adi Guru Shiva tells Parvati the Ram Mantra. It has all three pillars of our faith in it. Shakti is the asker, Shiva is the teller, and Vishnu is the subject.

Shiva tells Parvati, "Beloved, just that one enchanting name 'Rama' has the value of a thousand names.'"

'Will you say that in Sanskrit, Guruji?' asked the grandfather. The family sat up straight and put its hands together in respect to receive the Ram Mantra.

'After I recite the Ram Mantra, I would like to softly say "Rama, Rama, Rama, Rama" for one minute, with my eyes closed. Will you join me?'

'We will.'

'Good,' said the guru and recited what Shiva told Parvati:

'Sri Rama Rama Rameti Rame Raame Manorame
Sahasra Nama tattulyam Rama Nama varaanane
Rama, Rama, Rama, Rama, Rama, Rama . . .'

After that brief, spontaneous meditation, they opened their eyes and smiled at each other.

The guru looked at the mother. 'I wonder if you know the song *Kanakambara kamalasana jagadakhila dhama* about Sri Rama? It's the whole Ramayana in just fourteen lines in Sanskrit . . . a very melodious twentieth-century bhajan. It's a Ramakrishna Mission favourite.'

'I know it!' said the child. 'Ma has sung it to me since I was a baby.'

'I was going to play it for us from my phone if you didn't know it,' said the guru. 'It's a good song to begin or end a meditation with. Won't you both sing it to us?'

'We will!' said the mother and after humming the opening notes to fix the pitch, she nodded at the child and they began to sing. Barely into the first line, they found that the father had joined in. The delighted elders clapped heartily when they finished.

'When did you learn that?' said the mother to the father.

'You often sing it to the child. I think I learnt it by just being around,' said the father.

'Such songs please Mahadev,' said the guru, thinking of his own childhood when his mother had sung it to him.

'Now please tell us about the Ganga. I know you have travelled a lot along her banks and spent time in the holy towns,' said the grandmother.

'Where do I begin?' said the guru. 'Can a mere mortal do justice to the Ganga without being carried off by a flood of cliché? She has six headstreams and five sacred confluences. She's the life-giver to the northern plains of the subcontinent. She brims with the soul waters of ancient belief. She's the play course of adventure-seekers.'

'She's a divine being. She's the hard-won fruit of steadfast human penance. She's an ecosystem that has degenerated into the great gutter of modern India—you see the problem? How do we begin to talk about this river of rivers?'

'But I can tell you some astonishing things about her. The Ganga Basin is spread over 1.1 million sq. km. It is home to a quarter of India's population, imagine that. It's an intricate web of tributaries and distributaries, of canals, waterways and run-offs.'

'An American architect and Fulbright Scholar called Anthony Acciavatti spent a decade mapping the Ganga Basin. He called it "the world's most engineered river basin" and a "water machine" closely interconnected with the monsoon.'

'If you take a long boat ride on the Ganga, the journey will seem, in some places, like the delicious river idyll described by Rabindranath Tagore in his novel *The Wreck*. You almost expect to encounter some little twenty-first century Kamala, like Tagore's charming heroine, exclaiming eagerly over a fine head of carp or a basket of purple eggplants, orange pumpkins, cluster beans and other garden bounty that is never allowed to wither on the vine but is quickly plucked and cooked at its dewiest and freshest.'

'Is that the book that was made into the film *Noukadubi*?' said the mother.

'Yes, *Noukadubi* is the original name of Tagore's book. I read the English translation long ago. It's my favourite novel by Tagore,' said the guru.

'Not *Gora* or *Chokher Bali*?' said the grandfather, interested.

'There's something special about *Noukadubi* for me,' said the guru.

'I love the short story *Kabuliwala*,' said the mother.

'Tagore's stories touch the heart,' said the grandmother.

'It ends sadly, but I'll read you *Kabuliwala*,' said the mother to the child.

'You'll like it, I think,' said the grandfather, 'and you've heard a few sad stories by now.'

'The saddest story today is probably the Ganga's,' said the guru. 'At its dirtiest, the holy river resembles a sewage pipe with the top off. Nobody could possibly want to drink its waters now at places where factories and people pour an endless stream of filth into the river.'

'Let's hope the big clean-up succeeds,' said the father.

'Did you know that the Ganga has another great river named after her? It's the Mekong in South-East Asia. Mekong means "Ma Ganga".'

'Wow, like Parvati and Phnom Penh!' said the father.

'Yes, amazing, is it not? Of all the towns on Ganga's banks, it is Kashi or Varanasi which made Ganga great. And Kashi itself was made great by Mahadev. He is worshipped in Kashi as Vishwanath, Lord of the World. As you know, every believing Hindu is supposed to make a pilgrimage to Kashi at least once. There are lots of boys in places very far away named "Kashi Vishwanath" because they were born after a momentous family pilgrimage to Kashi.'

'In fact, in the old days, when people from other parts of India set out to Kashi, they said their final goodbyes at home because it was so far away and the journey to and fro was so dangerous and difficult. But go they did. Everyone was so emotionally invested in Kashi that they risked their lives for millennia to get there. So, in actual fact, what makes Kashi great is the living river of believers who come to see Mahadev. They could have a dip anywhere along the Ganga, you know, or in a local river, since all rivers are holy. So more than Ganga, it is really Mahadev who draws us all to Kashi.'

'Nearly thirty years ago I wondered if I, too, would find a personal connection with Kashi.'

'I took a boat to the other bank to see the panorama of ghats along the river. I saw tough-looking men with big muscles and moustaches who could only be wrestlers. They were the spiritual descendants of the *malla* of Krishna's days, like Chanura.'

'The ancient *akhara* or wrestling belt stretches across the *doaba* of the Ganga and Yamuna. It covers many old kingdoms and republics of the Upper Gangetic Basin. In epic times, the little kingdom of Kashi was ringed by Kosala to its north, Magadha to its east and Vatsa to its west. Wrestling is a historic local passion at Varanasi and across these old lands.'

'Looking at that long line of ghats slung across the riverfront, I was overwhelmed by the intense continuity of Kashi. All the people who lived in my head had come here or lived here—Shiva, Shakti, Nandi and Raja Harishchandra.'

'Adi Sankara came to Varanasi arguably between the fifth and the eighth century CE and they say he was taught a lesson in spiritual humility by none other than Mahadev himself.'

'Varanasi was Sant Kabir's hometown in the fifteenth century, and in the sixteenth century, Goswami Tulsidas composed the *Ramcharitmanas* and the *Hanuman Chalisa* here.'

'The Sikh Gurus greatly cherished Varanasi. Guru Nanak came here in 1506, went to the then Kashi Vishwanath temple, met with the pandits of Kashi to discuss his views and collected the verses of Kabir and other local saint-poets.'

'The sixth Guru, Guru Hargobind, sent an important emissary to Kashi to spread his teachings and the ninth

Guru, *Chadar-e-Hind* Guru Tegh Bahadur, visited Kashi twice.'

'His son, Gobind Rai, when barely six, came by with his mother while on a journey across north India, and as Guru Gobind Singh, the tenth Guru, sent five followers to Varanasi to learn Sanskrit.'

'In 1839, Maharaja Ranjit Singh covered the spires of the new Kashi Vishwanath temple with gold. This is the temple we see today, which was rebuilt in 1780 by Maharani Ahilyabai Holkar.'

'Swami Dayanand Saraswati, founder of the Arya Samaj, Sri Ramakrishna Paramahamsa and Swami Vivekananda showed up, too, on Kashi's ghats.'

'Almost every community and religious sect in India is represented in Kashi by its own temple, rest house and community hall. Kashi is also headquarters for a number of sanyasi sects.'

'There are those who came to Kashi to die a "holy death" with the surety of salvation, so death itself is known as "Kashi Labh", the "Profit of Kashi".'

'For at least three millennia, Hindu pilgrims have carried away a sealed pot of Ganga water to their corner of the continent, to keep in their prayer room.'.'

'Every time there is a death in the family, the seal is broken and a few precious drops of *Gangajal* are poured into the dying person's mouth for his or her salvation. As somebody always goes on pilgrimage to Kashi, the pots have been steadily replaced by each generation. So Ganga is literally found in every Hindu home across India and wherever Hindus go.'

'The modern satirical poet "Bedhab" Banarasi joked, "*Bedhab kabhon na chhodiyo aisi Kashi dham/Marne pe Ganga miley, jeete langra aam*—Never leave a place like Kashi, Bedhab, where dying, you have the benefit of the Ganga, and alive you may feast on langra mangoes".'

'The snack stalls of Kashi sell hot puris, potato curry and chutney. You could wash it down with cold, creamy lassi and top it with a Benarasi *paan*.'

'Indeed, the pilgrim party never stops along the Ganga. It begins at its icy Himalayan source, Gomukh, with offerings of flowers.'

'As the Ganga makes her way down from the snowline to the pine forests, the pilgrim presence picks up volume with sacred chants at the ashrams at Rishikesh. While the soul-seekers meditate, chant and pray at these ashrams on the riverbank, another kind of party goes on in the river itself.'

'Hooting and hollering, river rafters and kayakers bounce on the Ganga between high, bronzed rocks, in and out of rapids with terrifying names like "Golf Course" and "Three Blind Mice". I, too, have been river-rafting on that stretch from Rishikesh to Haridwar, to experience the Ganga's wild, joyful dance as she tumbles down through the mountains and enters the plains.'

'From Haridwar, she turns wide and slow as she proceeds further and further across the endless hot and dusty plains, eastwards to Bengal and the sea. Hindus say that she swells as she flows with the increasing load of human sin that is washed away in her.'

'The meeting of the Ganga with the sea at journey's end is considered a mystic moment. However, in a quirky link with the English who founded Kolkata on the Ganga's estuary, I experienced the river not from a pilgrim place but from a river warden's boat. The river warden or river pilot wore a white uniform and a black kepi and his face was wrinkled around the eyes from years of peering intently at the river and its banks, taking in all sorts of details that others would probably not notice. He knew every inch of the river on his stretch, every rock hidden in the riverbed, every shifting sand bank, every tide.'

'"Do you pray to the Ganga?" I ventured to ask when a silent camaraderie was established after twenty minutes or so of peacefully watching the river. It was the sort of question I could ask a fellow-Indian, even a stranger, without being considered intrusive.'

'The warden grinned. "I am a child of this river, as much as any Bhishma," he said. "To tell you the truth, I feel I *am* the Ganga, as though I had flowed down from Mahadev's head. I'm a part of her while alive, see? And one day my ashes will float on her waves and disappear into her."'

'He made me feel very close to Mahadev, this modern child of the Ganga.'

12

Tandavan

'I went with the family to a dance recital last evening, Guruji,' said the father, the next time they met. 'The theme was Mahadev as Nataraja, that he danced the Ananda Tandav at Chidambaram. It was a dance of joy to enlighten and sustain the world, they said. They mentioned the *Chidambara Rahasya* or "Secret of Chidambaram". Shiva is the Akash Lingam there; he is "formless as the sky" or is "consciousness vast as the sky". But it's also where we find his most famous form, the Nataraja. You keep mentioning Chidambaram. Can you tell us a story about it?'

'Do you want something on Nataraja?'

'We looked up Nataraja on the net, what his raised foot means and so on. It's about *Shiva jnana* overcoming ignorance and taking us to salvation, isn't it, which you explained last week?'

'That's right, it's the same message expressed through the statue.'

'I also read the history of Chidambaram on Wikipedia, that it was a royal Chola town and so on. But it doesn't satisfy me,' said the father.

'Why is that so?'

'It's because of your stories. There are more tales about Mahadev's devotees out south. We in the north don't seem to have had that many personal interactions with him in a long time. Why is that? His shivalas are around us and his yatras are most important to us. We love him so much. We can't do without him.'

'I saw something so touching the other day,' said the mother. 'It was painted on the back of an autorickshaw: "*Bhole Shankar bhool na jaana, Iss paapi se door na jaana*— Don't forget me, Bhole Shankar, don't go too far away from this sinner",' said the grandmother softly. 'Immortal words.'

'That's a good example of what I mean,' said the father. 'We totally love him. However, we seem to *know* him only at two extremes—one, at the level of the grand cosmic kathas, and two, at the level of our personal rituals, prayers and fasts.'

'I did say when we began that it's not possible to know everything about him,' smiled the guru. 'Pushpdanta said so long ago in the *Shiva Mahimna Stotra*.'

'Yes, but out south, he hasn't retreated permanently to Kailash after killing puranic demons. There seems to be a big middle ground between katha and personal ritual where he's remained hands-on. The way you tell it, he's been openly involved in the lives of regular people.

That's a new experience. I liked Nakkeeran. If I ever go to Madurai, it won't feel alien because I'll know what Mahadev was up to out there. I feel I know something special about Tripura and Manipur, too. The thing is that they made such a big deal of Chidambaram last evening that I want more than kings and cosmic theory. I want Mahadev in person.'

'Ah, so you noticed. The Shaiva tradition is immense and deep in south India. I told you about the *Tevaram*, the first seven books of a gigantic "Shaiva bible" that begins in the seventh century. They have sixty-three ancient Shaiva saints in Tamil Nadu alone, plus Mani Vasakar who wrote a big book called the *Tiru Vasakam* in the ninth century, it's a Shiv Puran. There's yet another huge book of *Shiv Lila*, about the games he played with ordinary people, just in Tamil Nadu. It has sixty-four stories in it.'

'If we go to Karnataka, we can spend hours with the Lingayats and Veerashaivas. Their HQ, as I may have mentioned, is in Andhra Pradesh at Srisailam temple. Then, in Kerala, the Shiva temple at Thrissur—which is actually Tiru Shiva Perur—is where Adi Shankara's parents prayed for a child.'

'Tiru means "Sri" across south India. So, for example, Tiruvananthapuram means "Sri Anantpur". And Thrissur or Tiru Shiva Perur means "Sri Shiv Mahapur". The ghee on the idol at the Thrissur shivala is over 800 years old and good for curing skin diseases. Vaids come to collect it for making medicine. Oh, the Deccan is chock-a-block with Shiva's presence. I have researched it for years in pursuit of him. If you want more of Mahadev in person, we'll go find him,' said the guru as they took their places for satsang and the opening call-and-response.

'This story is about something Mahadev did at Chidambaram,' began the guru. 'Back in the sixteenth century, in the year 1525 in fact, a family of musicians looked forward to the birth of a child. They were instrumental musicians who served at temples and their community was known as Isai Vellalar, literally "those who grow music". This family lived in the town of be Sirkazhi in the Kaveri Delta. They revered Mahadev as Koothan the Cosmic Dancer at his temple in Chidambaram, which was across the river Kollidam from Sirkali.'

'If they had a boy, the family planned to name him after Lord Shiva as "Tandavan", the "One who Dances the Tandav". The Tandav, as you know, is a philosophical concept expressed through bronze statues of Mahadev dancing.'

'But the child, when he arrived, was a terrible disappointment to his family. He was weak, sickly and unappealing. He was unable to eat properly, and did not grow strong. It was a handsome family, proud of its musical talent and its honourable place at the temple and in society. They were ashamed and angry that their son, their heir, he who should have made everyone envy them, was a liability, not an asset. He was clearly unfit to become a temple musician and a person of note. So Tandavan's position in his family, which should have been sky-high because he was the son, fell to the bottom because he was sickly.'

'All this open disapproval took its toll on the boy's nerves. He developed a severe skin infection all over his body. Pustules oozed from him and not even powders from the brilliant local Siddha healer or baths in medicinal water boiled with neem leaves could rid him of the hideous rashes. His family began to absolutely loathe him and the little boy grew even more sickly and silent.'

'His only friend was a musical neighbour, the lady of the house next door. Her name was Shivabhagyam, which means "Good Fortune". She always had a kind word for Tandavan. She invited him home to watch when she did her daily puja to Shiva and sang him many songs about Mahadev. Nobody liked her doing so but the lady insisted that it was both her right and her duty, and they lacked the nerve to oppose her.'

'Shivabhagyam's family was even better off than Tandavan's and Tandavan's family hated that she was good to him. They took it as a personal affront. How could they stop it? They came up with the diabolical idea of throwing him out of the house. If he no longer lived with them, he could not visit next door. Nor would the *kaaval* or police let anyone loiter on a residential street.'

'Driven out of home with abuses and curses by his own parents, the boy's precarious world wholly tumbled down around his ears. He gathered such shreds of dignity as were left to him and silently made his way to the big Shiva temple at Sirkali. Where do we go but to God's gates in such a situation?'

'Think of Surdas, born in 1478, forty-seven years before Tandavan. Sur was so cruelly ill-treated by his own family for being born blind that he left home in the wake of a band of wandering singers when he was just six or so.

They fed the child at the village where they stopped for the night but didn't want to be burdened with him. They slipped away while he slept. Can you imagine the child's terror when he woke up alone? His few brief hours of being accepted were over. Luckily he had a good singing voice which won him local sympathy. A kind lady in that village looked after him for some time. Sur found his final refuge in everybody's darling, Krishna, at Vrindavan. Swami Vallabhacharya provided for Sur, who died in 1573. If we look at Sur's verse, it's heart-breaking how he keeps calling Krishna "*Nand ke dulhare*" for he himself was nobody's child, like Tandavan.'

'Tandavan sat down at the very end of the ranks of beggars outside Shiva's temple. Unwilling to hold his hand out to anyone, he subsisted on such scraps of prasad as fell to him or the bananas or pieces of coconut and jaggery dropped before him by some passing pilgrim. He grew sicker by the day.'

'One hot afternoon, he crawled for shade into the temple's storeroom where the palanquins were kept. They were used to take images of Shiva and Parvati around in procession on big festival days. The thick stone walls of the temple storeroom made a cool cave. Weak with hunger, the boy fell asleep in a corner. After the evening worship was over, the priests put out the oil lamps and torches and locked up for the night, not knowing about the unconscious refugee in the storeroom. Waking up in the dark after an hour or so, Tandavan called out in a faint voice and lay back exhausted.'

'By and by a little girl appeared, carrying a tray which bore an oil lamp, a bowl of rice and vegetables and a small waterpot. She called out in a bright, affectionate way to Tandavan. Peering timidly out from behind a palanquin, he saw that it was the priest's little daughter. She fed and comforted the boy and as she turned to leave, advised him to go every day to Chidambaram. She told him to compose a new song to Shiva with the first words he heard spoken in the temple each day. Greatly cheered, Tandavan went to sleep.'

'Next morning when the storeroom was unlocked, Taandavan stepped out apologizing humbly to the priests for having fallen asleep in there. But the priests looked at him open-mouthed in awe. Gone were the wounds, gone was his loathsome skin and his sickly appearance. Not only was he healed but his skin now glowed with such lustre that they named him "Mutthu Tandavar". "Mutthu" means "pearl" from the Sanskrit word "mukta" and they gave him the respectful "r" at the end of his name.'

'But when Tandavan told them the night's incidents, nobody knew who the little girl with the tray was. The priest's daughter had stayed snug at home the previous evening. The boy looked in wonder at his soft, clear skin and felt sure it must have been Parvati, worshipped in Sirkali as Lokanayaki, the Heroine of the World, who had come in disguise to revive and console him.'

'The priests invited him to make his home in the temple's rest house. Tandavan gladly accepted. He said he would come back every day but had taken a vow to go to Chidambaram early each morning. He did not share the reason just then, afraid that he was incapable of composing even one song.'

'With a heartfelt salute to the gods at Sirkali, Tandavan crossed the river Kollidam to the Kanaka Sabha or Golden Hall, which was a part of the Shiva temple at Chidambaram.'

"*Bhuloka Kailayagiri Chidambaram!*" That was the first thing he heard at the temple. It was an exclamation by an ecstatic devotee as he walked in, meaning "Chidambaram is Mount Kailash on earth!"'

'Tandavan closed his eyes and prayed hard to Shiva for inspiration. Suddenly, a great light filled his head. His mouth opened by itself and a beautiful song poured out of him, starting with the first words he had heard in the temple. Everyone around him stopped to listen. Even the priests came out of the sanctum to hear him.'

'When the song ended, Tandavan flung himself down on the temple floor in reverence to Shiva. The people around him complimented him on the song. The priests gave him *vibhuti* and stepped back into the sanctum.'

'But the moment they stepped in, they called out in great surprise.'

'Five gold coins of great antiquity had mysteriously appeared at Shiva's feet.'

'The priests asked everybody which one of them had made the offering. But nobody could tell. Had a rich merchant made the offering, unnoticed? But why had he chosen to stay silent when the questioning began? Was it perhaps from a devout thief who had quietly given the Dancer a portion of his loot as penance? But nobody was seen going in, so who had placed those gold pieces in the sanctum?'

'The priests and everyone else present concluded that it was Shiva himself who had invisibly placed the gold coins at his own feet in appreciation of Tandavan's song. It was just like Shiva to do something so quirky and generous. The priests offered the gold coins to Tandavan but strangely, he refused to take them and went off to do pradakshina, smiling as if at a very dear and delightful thought.'

'What the puzzled priests and the public did not know was that Shiva had worked more than a miracle for Tandavan. He had mended Tandavan's broken heart.'

'Parvati had healed Tandavan's body and Koothan Shiva had let everyone know by his lila that Tandavan was as good as anyone. Shiva had shown the same generosity to this lonely beggar boy that he had shown the snakes when they came weeping to him, that he had shown the entire world by drinking the Kalakuta poison. Tandavan had no need to feel like an orphan now. The mother and father of the universe were with him.'

'Many songs followed after that and Tandavan sincerely kept his daily tryst with the Dancer. Once, when the Kollidam was in furious spate and he was unable to cross, he sang in despair, "The day has been wasted that I can't see you". The story goes that the floodwaters receded and let him cross.'

'One morning, to his great confusion, not a word was spoken in the temple. All Tandavan could hear was his own heartbeat pounding in his ears. He cried aloud, "*Peysaadey nenjamey!*" meaning, "Don't speak, my heart!" And so he composed the day's song with his own words.'

'His creative dependence on others was over.'

'Serene in his own strength now, Tandavan left his traumatic childhood behind.'

'He often wondered, though, about the transformative night in the Sirkali temple storeroom. He had almost died that night, at the very end of his tether. He had given up wholly on earthly ties and cast himself upon fate. Shiva and Parvati had taken pity on him.'

'Free in his mind now, happy in his music and poetry, grateful for his food and shelter and deeply pleased that his songs were appreciated, Tandavan found that he had no anger or grief left about those who had been so unkind to him. They became as unreal to him as if they were people met by another person in another life, though he did not hold back from meeting his friend Shivabhagyam.'

'But the townsfolk were greatly drawn to him, sure of a kind word. Knowing that he had suffered himself, they were not afraid to let down their guard and let him see their vulnerability.'

'At least sixty of Tandavan's songs are known to have survived and some of them are very famous. They are sung and danced to, even today.'

'The legend further says that one day, in the year 1600, a great light shone in Shiva's sanctum at Chidambaram. Mutthu Tandavar, an old man by then, walked right into that light and disappeared into it.'

'Aptly, it was the anniversary of the day that Shiva first danced the Ananda Tandav at Chidambaram.'

13

Mahadevi

Since the mother had a holiday from work, she joined the grandfather and guru for tea on one of the guru's unofficial visits. 'Are there no stories about women devotees, Guruji?' she asked. 'I've been meaning to ask you this. I know we have a heavy patriarchal tradition, but I'm one of those who wants to push for change from within. Like my family here, I hate it when someone discriminates by caste and gender. New India cannot live by the rules of old patriarchy any longer. But I won't give up the gods. I would be lost without them.'

'Absolutely. God doesn't believe in caste and gender. But society has been selfishly slow to change. Nor has the vote-bank politics of decades helped the process. About women saints . . . I have the impression that the common link between them is that they all faced cruelty. All except for the girl-saint Andal in the eighth century, who was in love with Vishnu. She is believed to have disappeared into Vishnu's image at the temple of Srirangam. Her poems to Krishna were a major influence, you know, on Sri Ramanuja. He was the tenth-century founder of the Srivaishnava movement, which swept the north like wildfire. Sant Ramanand of Kashi was his follower; Sant Kabir was Ramanand's disciple and so on and so on, including Tulsidas. That means little Andal was a person of great influence in Indian history. But our textbooks don't tell us that a girl child inspired a great and lasting religious and social reform movement.'

'Karaikal Ammayar, "the old lady of Karaikal", is the earliest woman saint I can think of. Her real name was Punitavati. She lived in the port city of Karaikal in the sixth century, in the old Chola country. She's one of the sixty-three ancient Tamil Shaiva saints, collectively called the Nayanmar. You'll find their statues in every major Shiva temple out there. She was a young woman devotee of Shiva and received a magic mango from him one day as a mark of his favour. Her husband, the merchant Paramadattan, refused to believe it and so she begged for another mango from Mahadev to convince her husband that she spoke the truth. When the second magic mango appeared, her husband could no longer think of Punitavati as his wife for now she seemed like a goddess to him. He moved to another town and married another woman.'

'Punitavati was devastated. She begged Mahadev to turn her at once into an ugly old woman. She then went all the way north to the Himalayas, God knows how, and climbed Mount Kailash upside down on her head and hands, for she did not want to disrespectfully put her feet on holy Kailash.'

'I found her story in English translation at the Sahitya Akademi library. It's in the book of Tamil Shaiva saints called *Periya Puranam.* The world must have seemed upside down to her, poor lady, that she had been deserted for being good.'

'What an extraordinary story to tell little girls, "Be good but just good enough",' said the mother, with a shiver.

'Sounds grim, does it? But the positive interpretation is very Shaiva. She was liberated from a lifetime of worldly ties and went off to God sooner rather than later. And what a blessing fell on her on Kailash!'

'Shiva asked her if she had another wish, and Punitavati asked for the most wonderful boon. She wanted to see Shiva and Parvati dance the Ananda Tandav *together*. Touched by her wish, the divine couple appeared to her in utmost beauty as Gauri-Shankar and actually danced for her on Kailash. What a darshan, what a darshan of darshans. How kind of them, our beautiful, dancing gods. If I am "jealous" of any devotee, it is of this Ammaji. What a blissful sight it must have been to see the father and the mother of the universe dance in joy for her! Punitavati was absorbed into their light at the end of the dance. The very sight of it gave her mukti. Here on earth, even though they respectfully show her as the old hag that she asked to become, they nevertheless save their finest silks for her statue in the long line-up of the sixty-three Nayanmar statues in big temples. It's their way of showing love even today to this person from 1400 years ago who loved Mahadev.'

'After that, I can think of Akka Mahadevi of Karnataka in the twelfth century and Lal Ded or Lalleshwari of Kashmir in the mid-fourteenth century. They became "women saints" after they were severely ill-treated by their in-laws. They left their families and actually wandered about naked in utter rejection of everything their societies stood for.'

'Going by their poetry, Akka and Lalla sound like gentle, affectionate young girls, who dreamed like any girl, of love and kindness. Akka was ten when she was married and Lalla was twelve. I'm told that the Kashmiri language is full of Lalla's sayings. Lalla had to eat last, alone in the kitchen, after everybody else. Her mother-in-law used to put a big stone on her plate and cover it with a layer of rice to make it look like a large helping. Her husband offered no support at all. Why was the mother-in-law so mean to a little girl? We don't know. Maybe she was mean because she had the power to be mean. But it's too easy to sneer that "women are women's worst enemies". If that is so, isn't it because their softer natures have been perverted over a long time by the social pressure to produce sons and quietly put up with bad behaviour as their duty?'

'Like Tandavan, both Akka and Lalla transferred all their love to Shiva. They wrote poems to Mahadev that people still recite.'

'And then, in the sixteenth century, we have the most famous woman saint of north India, Mira Bai, who suffered so much because of her unswerving love for Krishna. Mira left home, too, although she was a royal Rajput widow of only thirty-eight years.'

'Medieval Marathi women saints like Jana Bai, who loved Krishna as Vitthala Pandurang at Pandharpur, did not have an easy time, either. Jana Bai was left as a child at the temple by her starving parents. Sant Namdev rescued her and took her home. She spent her whole life as a servant to his family, although she became a much-loved poet herself.'

'Then there was Mukta Bai, the younger sister of Sant Jnaneshwar. She and her three brothers were orphaned and faced a lot of social persecution. It could seem at first like a long tale of sorrow in which these women saints sublimated their suffering into God-love.'

'Yet, when I hear a Marathi abhang like "*Namdev kirtan kari, premabhara naatse Panduranga*", all doubts and questions vanish. All I can sense is Krishna dancing in joy when Namdev sings to him. How do you explain that?'

'When I show up at Banke Bihariji's temple in Mathura, I feel Surdas and Swami Vallabhacharya by my side. I go to a corner to sit looking at Krishna and find myself humming Vallabhacharya's song, "*Madhuram, madhuram, Mathuradipatey akhilam madhuram*—sweet, sweet, everything is sweet about the Lord of Mathura".'

'I find myself humming "*Vanamali Vasudeva, Vanamohana Radharamana, Shashi-vadana Sarasija-nayana, Jaganmohana Radharamana*"—Dark One, garlanded with wild flowers, with your face as bright as the moon, and eyes like lotus petals, enchanter of Radha . . . enchanter of all.'

'I chant "*Radhey-Radhey, Radhey-Radhey, Radhey-Govinda, Brindavana Chandra, Anathanatha Deenabandho, Radhey-Govinda*", and I feel an ecstasy possess me and my eyes overflow.'

'If the gods call you, you have to go, you know. It's such a strong tug at the heart that you just have to go, and you throw your arms up for refuge if you get to see them. Darshan is what the gods give you by their grace. It's not something you "take"; it's something you "receive" with gratitude.'

'Then, when I see an audience of ten thousand people at Tirupati spontaneously getting up to dance during a bhajan evening by Vittaldas Maharaj—thousands of regular people, mind you, of all castes and classes, dancing joyfully together with the firm conviction that Krishna is dancing with them, what am I to make of it? There's so much positive energy in the air that I want to be part of it. I get up and dance, too. God-love overpowers me, which fills me with affection for everyone around. My heart turns soft as butter.'

'It sounds totally uplifting,' said the mother rapturously, clasping her hands. 'We must go, too, with the child. Now please tell us more about Akka Mahadevi.'

'Wasn't she a Veerashaiva?' said the grandfather. 'I've read her poems long ago, translated by A.K. Ramanujan.'

'Yes, it's a powerful tale. "Akka" means "elder sister" in Kannada, Marathi, Telugu and Tamil. She was called that later in life. The name she was given at birth was "Mahadevi", meaning, of course, "Parvati".'

'Akka was born to a rich Hindu family in Udutadi village. It's in present-day Shimoga district in Karnataka. She was married off at the age of ten to a man named Kausika, who was a Jain chieftan. The Jains, then as now, were a prosperous community and Akka was expected to live the life of a medieval "corporate wife"—to dress well, bear her husband sons and fulfil her traditional biological, domestic, social and ritual duties. Instead, Akka ran away.

Moreover, she cast off her clothes, possibly influenced by the Digambara or "sky-clad" sect of naked Jain ascetics, and wore her long hair as her only covering.'

'What made a young, gently bred girl reject her prescribed life and wander bravely alone into the aggressive, jeering world of men? We cannot begin to imagine what she must have endured, or the strength of mind and conviction she had to make and live by this terrifying choice. And in those days! We can understand why Punitavati wanted to be turned at once into an old woman.'

'Akka loved Shiva as "Mallikarjuna", her "Lord white as jasmine", the way Andal and Mira loved Krishna. This love poured out in about 350 vachanas or sayings in Kannada. After wandering around alone for some time, Akka wished to join a "soul family" of Shaivas.'

'The Veerashaivas were a new and radically democratic group of Hindus in the region. She made her way to their camp at a place called Kalyana and asked to be one of them.'

'Scandal had preceded her and she must have presented an unsettling sight; young, staunch and unclad. Allama Prabhu, the Veerashaiva leader, was caught between his heartfelt Shaiva empathy with all creatures and this severe test of his belief. Did "all creatures" include a woman who'd broken so many male rules? Despite his great saintliness and impeccable credentials as a spiritual democrat, this democracy did not automatically include single, independent women. Instead we see the overpowering need of the male mind to build a social context for Akka's "wildness", to fit her into society as "God's wife" if not man's. This is how tradition reports the encounter.'

'Allama Prabhu asked Akka, "Who is your husband?"'

'Akka answered, "I am married forever to Mallikarjuna."'

'Allama Prabhu said: "Why do you roam around naked as though illusion can be peeled off by mere gestures? And yet you wear a sari of hair? If the heart is free and pure, why do you need it?"'

'Akka said, with absolute honesty: "Until the fruit is ripe inside, the skin will not fall off." By "fruit" she meant that her mind was not ready yet.'

'Melted by her sincerity, Allama Prabhu accepted Akka into the Veerashaiva fold. But after some years, while merely in her twenties, when Akka left to look for Mallikarjuna. Not one person supported her. The tale goes that she went to the holy peak of Srisailam. Did I tell you that it's in Kurnool district in Andhra Pradesh? Adi Shankara meditated under an ancient banyan tree at Srisailam and composed the *Shivananda Leheri* there.'

'It's possible that Akka was eaten by a tiger in the jungle. Her body was never found. I can't bear to think of it. Alas, there are many child brides in our land even today. Nine hundred years after her, in the twenty-first century, little girls are still being married off early all over India although it's against the law.'

'It's an astounding story,' said the mother, 'and I take your point about the little girls.'

'I often wonder at the behaviour of our ancestors—and some of our contemporaries,' said the grandfather. 'I want to like them more than I do but it's not so easy. Sometimes I feel no connection with them for the cruel things they do, although they are my own people. It's the exact opposite of what I feel for the wonderful gods they worshipped and handed over to us all. I can never break with the gods. They are too beautiful and they go too deep.'

'Yes, that's how it seems to work for me,' said the mother. 'You can say anything to me about my attitude and behaviour as a Hindu and I will sincerely try to correct myself if your accusations are truthful. But the minute someone insults or mocks the gods, I find that I've switched off in my head.'

'It's complicated all right,' said the guru, 'and my guess is that you're doing exactly what other moderate, peaceful, progressive Hindus do. Being Hindu the way we understand it is the new "love that dares not speak its name". Never mind, I'll tell you some nice, cheerful stories about Shiva next time.'

At their next gathering, the guru looked fondly at the father.

'I kept thinking of what you said—that you wanted more of Mahadev in person. Today, I want to share some other tricks he played to support those who loved him.'

'I love him too!' said the child.

'Yes, I know you do. And I'm sure he loves you. It's because of you that we're here together to talk about him.'

'Well, once upon a time, Varaguna Pandyan was the king of the Pandyas with his capital at Madurai. He was a strong, sincere king who ruled his subjects with affection and justice.'

'At that time, Hemnath, a gifted singer and veena player from somewhere to the north of Madurai, went around from kingdom to kingdom, challenging all the best musicians of the land to compete in music with him. It was a point of honour not to refuse, so of course, nobody could say no. Hemnath was not only a brilliant artiste but also had great presence. He was a fine figure of a man who dressed very well and presented himself with great confidence. He had a troupe of accompanists, all trained to the pitch of perfection, that went everywhere with him. He looked like a king himself when he sat down to sing in a king's court. Many singers lost their nerve just looking at him and were defeated. Hemnath always walked out the winner.'

'He arrived grandly in Madurai to challenge its musicians. He spoke arrogantly and boastfully. Now, Madurai was a proud city. Its people were very artistic and talented, as you've heard, and had a very good opinion of themselves. Here was a worthy challenge. Varaguna Pandyan asked for a song from Hemnath to exhibit his skill to Madurai. Hemnath, with a wave of his hand, made his disciples play a tune instead. They were so good that everyone grew worried. Bhanabhadra, the court musician, was very good, too. But if Hemnath's accompanists were so skilled, what would the master-singer be like?'

'The competition was fixed for the next morning. The king took Bhanabhadra aside to ask him if he could defeat Hemnath and save Madurai's honour, and Bhanabhadra promised faithfully to do his best.'

'That night, Bhanabhadra, who worshipped Mahadev as Lord Somasundara, prayed as he never had before: "Please help me defeat Hemnath. I am not at all confident that I can do this on my own. I badly need your grace".'

'Mahadev decided to help him and also have some fun. He assumed the form of a woodcutter. For an extra touch, he made his hair grey. He tied rags around his head and body, hefted a great bundle of firewood out of nowhere and plucked a fine veena out of thin air. Carrying both, he made his way to the guest house where Hemnath and his troupe had been housed by the king. He made himself comfortable on the verandah of the guest house. He yawned, stretched and loudly hummed a few notes. These noises disturbed Hemnath, who woke up irritated.'

'Meanwhile, the woodcutter began to play the veena. Such heavenly notes poured into Hemnath's room that he froze in wonder. Soon, whoever was outside began to sing a melodious song in a raga never heard before. Hemnath could not bear the suspense. He came out and was shocked to see a shabby woodcutter on the verandah.'

'"Hey, woodcutter! Who are you, man?" he said.'

'The woodcutter stopped his music. "I? I'm a servant of Bhanabhadra, the court-singer of Varaguna Pandyan. He shared his music with me. But when I grew old, my master said I had better stop singing and playing. He said I was not up to the mark. So I play well away from him, whenever the fit takes me."'

'Hemnath asked the woodcutter to sing again, which he did, bringing tears to Hemnath's eyes. The woodcutter then took leave of Hemnath and disappeared into the night.'

'Hemnath thought frantically to himself, "I have never heard this raga before. This is no raga known to man. It's a divya raga. If that old fellow, a servant, could sing a divine raga so well, what must his master be like? I cannot face Bhanabhadra. Let me leave Madurai at once."'

'Hemnath woke up his troupe, made them pack swiftly and left town in the middle of the night.'

'Mahadev then appeared in a dream to Bhanabhadra and said: "Don't worry! I took the form of a wood-cutter, sat on the verandah of the guest house where Hemnath stayed and played some music. He left Madurai at midnight."'

'When Bhanabhadra woke up, he went as always to the temple and worshipped Lord Somasundara before going to the king's court. The king sent a servant to fetch Hemnath. The servant looked all over the place until the people who lived next door told him, "All we know is that a woodcutter came to the guest house verandah and sang. After that, we saw Hemnath leave at midnight". The servant went back and reported this quietly to Varaguna Pandyan in an ante-room at the palace.'

'The king called for Bhanabhadra and asked, "Could you tell me what you did after you left me?"'

'Bhanabhadra said, "Your Majesty, I went home and prayed to Lord Somasundara to help me defeat Hemnath. He appeared in my dream and said, 'Don't worry! I took the form of a woodcutter, sat on the verandah of the guest house where Hemnath stayed and played some music. He left Madurai at midnight'".'

'Varaguna Pandyan realized at once that this was a lila by Mahadev. He gave Bhanabhadra many rich presents and said, "Our Lord God is truly the servant of those who love him. May you sing his praise for many years!"'

'Imagine Shiva bending the rules like that. How eccentric of him! Is this from the book of sixty-four stories?' said the father.

'Yes. The book is called *Tiru Vilayadal*, which means "Sacred Games". Shiva did two things in this lila. He not only saved a devotee's honour but also taught an arrogant man a lesson in humility. He is known to do that. He disguised himself as a humble labourer in Kashi and put himself in the path of none other than Adi Shankara, the master philosopher, our beloved Acharya himself.'

'Shankara was a fearless child prodigy and found many admiring followers in Kashi. Perhaps Mahadev thought he needed a reality check at that point? One day, on his way to bathe in the Ganga, Acharya found his path blocked by this labourer and automatically waved him away.'

'"What should I move?" said the labourer sweetly, "my body, which is made of the same five elements as yours or my immortal soul, which is exactly the same in me as in you? Is there a difference between the reflection of the sun in the Ganga and its reflection in the ditch in the quarters of the labourers?"'

'Acharya knew at once who stood before him and fell at his feet, grateful for the lesson. The labourer vanished and they say that Acharya instantly composed five verses about this conversation that we know today as the *Manisha Panchakam*—the Five Verses of Conviction.'

'Mahadev doesn't spare anyone, does he, however great?' said the father.

'Nor does he hold back from helping the humblest and weakest. Such a lila is like medicine to cure us of false pride—he doses us with the mercy of *Shiva jnana*.'

'When our own tradition teaches us not to discriminate, why didn't people learn from it?' said the mother in anguish.

'Too many people across society found it convenient not to learn,' said the grandfather. 'Parts of society have still to catch up with the Constitution.'

'Found what convenient?' said the child.

'Would you like to hear another story?' said the guru, leaving it up to the family to explain the unhappy topic when it chose to the child, since she had never heard her family speak about or comment on 'caste' or 'outcaste' and both her parents and grandparents had friends from many communities who comfortably visited their home.

'Yes, please!' said the child, diverted.

'This lila is celebrated every year at a place called Puttu Thopu in Madurai city in the month of Shravan, which is also special to Shiva elsewhere in India. Puttu Thopu is located on the south bank of the Vaigai. They say that this is the place where Mahadev performed one of those sixty-four lilas. This happened in the ninth century.'

'Varaguna Varman the Second, the Pandya king of the time, ordered every household in Madurai to help build a massive bund on the banks of the Vaigai to protect the kingdom from floods in the monsoon. A poor old lady called Vanti Amma was ordered by the overseer to carry baskets of soil as her task. But she was too weak and old for it. She had no family and could not pay anyone to take her place. However, if she did nothing at all, the guards would make her pay a hefty fine, or worse, send her to jail for dereliction of duty. Pandyan law was strict. Mani Vasakar, the king's trusted minister, though a saint, had been put in jail for misusing state funds to build a private temple to Shiva. Devotion was one thing. State funds belonged to the state.'

'So Vanti Amma, who prayed every day to Mahadev as her lifelong saviour, gamely came up with a scheme that she dedicated to him. She counted out a few coins from her scant hoard and went shopping, after which she carefully prepared some puttu, mixing coarsely ground rice, grated coconut, jeera, salt and water, which she steamed in bamboo cylinders. She planned to offer portions of this puttu to anyone who would help her.'

'Mahadev, who was idly watching the people of Madurai scurry around like ants, noticed her activities. He understood her plan at once and liked the genuine effort that the old lady was making to do her duty and save her dignity. "She deserves some help, see how she's trying to cope alone," he told Parvati and promptly thought of a new game to play.'

'Vanti Amma sat near the riverbank with the fresh puttu enticingly laid out on a banana leaf. She waved a palm-leaf fan over it to keep flies away and also fan herself.'

'"Puttu for any good person who will work in my place!" she called.'

'But everybody who passed by was already on embankment duty and Vanti Amma grew nervous. Would nobody come forward? Would she have to go to jail, after all?'

'After some time, a boy of not more than fifteen or sixteen, dressed in a faded dhoti, came by, stopped and greeted her.'

'"I'm very hungry, Granny. Won't you give me some puttu?" he said, eyeing the savoury white logs.'

'"Do take some, child," said the old lady.'

'"Why are you giving away free puttu, Granny?" said the boy, squatting beside her.'

'"Child, I don't have the strength to do my share of the work. So I'm hoping somebody will take my place in exchange for some food," said Vanti Amma.'

'"Oh, is that all? I can do that for you," laughed the boy, flexing his strong, young arm.'

'"May Somasundara bless you! Take as much puttu as you like," said the old lady happily.'

'The boy delicately helped himself to just a handful of puttu. After eating it, he smacked his lips and grinned cheekily.'

'"Excellent puttu, Granny. Maybe I'll come back for more," he said and strolled off towards the guards to pick up a stout cane basket.'

'"I'm standing in for that old lady, see? Better tick her name off your list," he told them and went to work on the embankment.'

'The boy carried soil steadily to and fro from the earthworks. Coming and going, he sang and whistled, made funny remarks, helpfully caught the arm of anyone who stumbled and cheerfully laboured side by side with the people of Madurai. The atmosphere around him grew light and carefree despite the hard work going on.'

'When the overseer gave his section a short break, the boy put the basket down under a tree, turned his back on the bustle and peacefully went to sleep.'

'Meanwhile, the king himself arrived to inspect the work. He was very annoyed to spot a teenager sleeping the morning away. He dismounted from his horse, strode up to the boy and delivered a smart blow of his cane on the boy's bare back.'

'"*Aaah!*" screamed the workers, even the king. They had all felt the lash. What strange miracle was this?'

'Now, Varaguna Varman was no fool. He was, after all the Pandyan king and knew something about the god he prayed to every day. Who else could it be, playing such tricks?'

'He fell to his knees besides the boy who turned over and smiled.'

'"I'm sorry it hurt. But it couldn't be helped, could it, when I'm in each one of you . . . even in old women with no strength to work?" he said and vanished.'

'The king could not believe his luck.'

'"I saw him. I actually saw him. He spoke to me!" he said joyfully, and taking the basket used by Mahadev, he reverently filled it with the soil on which Mahadev had slept to take back to his puja room at the palace.'

'But before he left, he excused Vanti Amma from work, presented her his big golden ring as a mark of respect and apology, and humbly requested her to pack the remaining puttu for him as prasad.'

'When the workers realized what had happened, they fell to their knees, thanking Mahadev for appearing in their midst. Those he had touched, joked with and teased could not believe their luck. "We must have done something good in our past lives that he showed himself to us so affectionately, as one of us," they said, eyes overflowing. They felt certain of good luck for the rest of their days and went back to work with great good will.'

'The bund came up very well with not one accident.'

'The old lady thanked Shiva, heart and soul. She died soon after in great peace and happiness, for Shiva gave her mukti for just that handful of puttu.'

'Krishna gave Sudama unimaginable wealth for two handfuls of poha. Shiva gave Vanti liberation itself for a handful of puttu. *Hari bhakti*, *Shiva jnana*. The gods love to serve those who love them.'

'I must tell you something nice here that unites the north and south in the most unexpected way. Guess what Yashoda Maiyya gave Krishna as packed lunch in Vrindavan? It was mixed rice or curd rice with pickle or chips, typically wrapped in a leaf-packet. No, I'm not making it up, how could I? It's in the *Srimad Bhagavatam*. Vyasa says, "*vame panau masrna kabalam tad phalanyangulishu*". "His left hand held the blob of mixed rice and between the fingers of the other, he held the accompaniment", when Krishna had lunch with the *gopa* boys while out grazing the cows.'

'The Kannada word for curd rice is *masaru anna*, as I discovered in Bengaluru, while Vyasa's word for mixed rice is *masrna*. So if we link it backwards, we could well say that the "mixed rice" was curd rice. There would have been no shortage of curds in Yashoda's home. We know how Krishna loved butter, milk and curds. The usual "accompaniment" to curd rice is pickle or chips, or both pickle and chips. The pickle could have been mango or lemon. The "chips" could have been papad or fried vegetable chips. To think we still eat the food our dear Lord ate!'

'Do you know, in the Telugu lands, they say *majjiga* for buttermilk? They call it "the mother of the motherless" for its comfort value. I don't wonder at it—milk and milk products were the old building blocks of our diet. Once upon a time, it was considered a sin against society to dilute the milk you sold, and we had strict rules about milking. The cows were grazed only on sweet organic grass and no cow could be milked until its calf had drunk its fill. The cowherd boys were carefully instructed on these matters.'

'How lucky were those *gopa* boys who innocently played all day with Krishna and Balarama . . . Sridama, Subala and Stoka were Krishna's three best friends by the Yamuna. Everywhere you look, you find them by a riverbank, a lake, a hill, the shore, celebrating the lila of the gods.'

'So you won't be surprised to know that every Shravan, to this day, the people of Madurai make puttu to take on a picnic to Puttu Thopu in remembrance of Mahadev's lila there. "Thopu" means "grove" or "thicket". The Meenakshi temple is closed for two days during that time so that Parvati and Shiva can go in procession to the banks of the Vaigai to join the party . . .'

'Imagine Mahadev romping around as an old woodcutter and a cheeky teen,' chuckled the father. 'And I liked his public gesture to Tandavan. Mahadev really is a play-actor—both at the big level of maya and in our small lives.'

'He's very soft-hearted for such a strong, masculine god,' said the grandmother. 'That must be his womanly side.'

'I found another story about Mahadev in which he became a woman. He did not ask Parvati to go in his place. He rushed to the rescue himself in the form of a mortal woman.'

'Mahadev as a woman?' said the father. 'That's unusual. We know that Shakti is his other half. We know that Vishnu became Mohini to save the situation after the Milk Ocean was churned. But I've never heard of Mahadev himself taking the form of a woman.'

'I was wrong in saying that all women devotees except Andal were tragic figures,' said the guru to the mother. 'Vanti was not tragic. She had a big problem that Mahadev more than solved. This story about Mahadev as a woman goes back a long way, it's even older than the story of how he carried earth for a handful of puttu. Would you like to hear it?'

'Of course,' said the mother.

'Mahadev's lila with Vanti and the puttu was in the ninth century. Over 200 years before that, in the late sixth century, a girl called Ratnavati was an ardent devotee of Mahadev, whom she worshipped by the name Sevadinath. She inherited this love from her father Ratnaguptan, who was a merchant and a man of faith. Ratnavati lived with her huband in Trichy. There were no elders or relatives at home; it was just the two of them and a part-time servant. The husband, being a merchant himself, was often away on work. When Ratnavati became pregnant, she prayed every day to Sevadinath Mahadev for the baby's health. She chanted slokas, did puja and offered bel leaves and milk. She firmly believed that Mahadev would protect her and her unborn child all the way.'

'But naturally, Ratnavati wanted her mother by her side during the birth. Nobody else would do. She sent word to her mother who lived some distance away from Trichy across the river Kaveri, to come to her before the birth. When the date drew near, Ratnavati's mother began to prepare her daughter's favourite snacks to take along. She also made the special restorative laddoos usually given to new mothers, some medicinal oil, some herbal marmalade called lehiyam that we call chyavanprash in the north and a big jar of pure ghee from cow's milk. Going to Trichy by bullock cart took two weeks those days and Ratnavati's mother set out with two attendants in time for the baby's expected arrival. But when they neared Trichy, they found to their great dismay that the Kaveri was in flood and totally impossible to cross.'

'While her mother fumed and fretted on the far bank of the Kaveri, Ratnavati went into early labour and began to panic. It was bad enough that her husband was away on work, planning to be back before the baby was due. But where on earth was her mother? As the sky grew dark and rain clouds began to empty on Trichy, she prayed desperately to Shiva, "Dear God, my saviour, my Lord Sevadinath, I know you have no parents but you do have two beautiful children on Kailash and all of us here are your children, too. I'm sure you understand how much I need my mother now. Please don't leave me alone, please help me".'

'Ratnavati had barely finished her prayer when she heard a knock on the door. There stood her mother, beaming, carrying many baskets and bundles. Relieved and happy, Ratnavati let her mother take charge. With her mother's able help, she delivered a beautiful baby. Her mother took over the house and knackily looked after the baby. She dosed Ratnavati with healing syrups, let her sleep undisturbed between feeds, cooked nourishing meals and kept the house fresh and tidy. She did not let Ratnavati pick up even a pot of drinking water. Ratnavati felt thoroughly petted and pampered by all this loving care.'

'After a few days, Ratnavati heard a knock and went to the door. She was shocked to see her mother and the two attendants.'

'My dear daughter, please forgive me for not coming to you sooner!' cried her mother. 'The Kaveri was flooded and I couldn't cross. How worried I was! I am so relieved to see you looking well. Where is my grandchild?'

'As her mother sobbed in relief, Ratnavati rushed to the kitchen where she had seen her mother's double go. But that mother was nowhere to be seen. Ratnavati looked at her mother in utmost wonder and went at once to the puja room to thank Mahadev. Who else could it have been? Sevadinath Mahadev had become a mortal mother for the sake of a girl who totally trusted him and called out to him in complete faith. He had even brought the same food and medicine that Ratnavati's mother had prepared.'

'Ratnavati dissolved in floods of grateful tears when she realized how perfectly Mahadev, the god of doctors, the Vaidishvar himself, had looked after her and the baby.

Throughout their lives, she and her mother would often break down remembering it. "Did Sevadinath really do such-and-such?" they would think and sit down abruptly, overcome by his maternal compassion. That Great God beyond time and space, without beginning or end, that Adi Guru, that Mahayogi, that demon-killer, that Trikaldarshi who could see the past, present and future seamlessly, was not remote to them. How could he be, when he had delivered Ratnavati's baby, plaited her hair for her, washed her clothes, cooked her food and fed her with his own hand as her mother?'

'Ratnavati and her family held a big puja of thanksgiving and invited the whole town to the feast to celebrate this miracle. Everyone was deeply touched by Mahadev's caring practical kindness. They loved him even more for this lila.'

"'What does he not do for us? He drank poison to save the world. He even became the mother to this girl in her hour of need," they said, shedding tears of wonder. From that day, Shiva was given the name "*Thayumanavar*", the Lord who even became the mother.'

'The people told their king, Mahendravarman Pallava the First, and he built a temple to Shiva as Thayumanavar in Trichy up on its big rock hill. The Pandya kings of the eighth century made the temple even bigger.'

'The emperors of Vijayanagar and after them the Nayak kings of Madurai rebuilt it in medieval times. That's how it's gone on for hundreds of years—Ratnavati's experience of *Ishakripa*, God's grace, is enshrined as the legitimate lore of the land in the temple that was built by Mahendravarman and kept up by king after king from succeeding dynasties.'

'They hold a festival there every year, even today in the twenty-first century, in which they enact this lila with great feeling and give medicinal oil as prasad to new mothers. Even to this day. They do this not only to remember Shiva's motherly mercy but to teach everyone who cares to learn that a man can be a mother. A man has it in him to be as caring and supportive as a mother if he tries. Mahadev, that most manly of gods, has set an example to all men.'

14

Shivaya

'A katha allows us to experience everything in four ways,' said the guru at the next gathering. 'First, as a lived experience when we listen; second, in the writing down of it; and third, in the rereading of it . . . and most crucially when we retell it and pass it on to new listeners, especially the young. That's how it's still alive. We've kept a tight hold on the katha and bhajan habit and moreover, we can tell our stories according to our times.'

'I like it that we can ask questions and that we don't have to defend the indefensible,' said the mother.

'Yes, that's one of the most attractive things about the tradition. It's like a flowing river, a *pravah*, not like water confined in a well,' said the grandfather.

'Speaking of which, we have something to show you, haven't we?' said the mother to the guru, with a look at the child.

The child got up and went to fetch a roll of chart paper, which she carefully unrolled for the guru.

'A map of our holy places, *Aa Setu Himalaya*!' exclaimed the guru. He studied it with deep attention and looked up, beaming.

'This is marvellous!'

'We wanted to set down our sacred geography for ourselves,' said the father.

'It's our family project. All five of us worked on it this week,' smiled the grandmother.

The guru looked again at the map.

'It's beautiful,' he said. 'A nice outline of India with snow peaks, hills, rivers, jungles, desert and oceans all lightly filled in as the background, and the tirthas and kshetras drawn boldly on top. I see you've done the different terrains in watercolour. That is the most difficult thing to do. You can't correct mistakes like you can with oil paint or acrylic. Who is the artist here?'

'It was a division of labour,' said the grandmother.

'As the engineer and draughtsman, I did the outline,' said the grandfather.

'My son filled in the geography. He did the watercolour work since he used to like drawing and painting,' added the grandmother.

'I was afraid that I was too out of practice. But I think it's like cycling or swimming, it comes back. My eyes and hand remembered the technique,' said the father.

'I marked the holy sites and then he drew and coloured the symbols—Shaiva, Vaishnava, Shakta, Kaumara and Ganapatya,' said the mother.

'And what did you do?' asked the guru to the child.

'Dadi and I made the list of place names. I checked all the spellings and Papa and Dadu wrote them,' said the child, unaware that she had been pleasantly set up, in the age-old way of mothers and fathers, to get some education from the exercise.

'It's come off very well. You should frame it,' said the guru. 'But before you frame it, I should like to have a scanned colour copy—perhaps an A4 sized one that I can take around to show my friends. You must all sign it for me.'

'Of course, we'll make copies for you. I'll do it before you leave. It's great that you like it, Teacher,' said the father.

'Do you plan to travel, Teacher?' said the mother.

'Yes, I do. And it's thanks to our katha sessions. The land calls me! I want to wander the pilgrim trails by foot, bus and train, wherever I feel called. I may be away for six months, if not more, so this will be our last session for a while,' said the guru.

'For that long? I'll miss you, Teacher!' cried the child.

'We'll miss you, too,' said the grandfather while the grandmother, father and mother looked at the guru in open dismay.

'I'll be back in no time,' said the guru. He looked at the mother.

'When I come back, may I teach the child Sanskrit myself? It's my "thank you" to her and to you all for starting me off on this journey. I feel strangely territorial about it. But no fee, that's my condition.'

'Guruji, would you, really? That would be so perfect. What a blessing,' said the mother, with a distinct wobble to her voice.

'I want to learn from you, Teacher,' said the child, jumping up. 'I don't want anyone else. Ma said we couldn't dare ask you to teach me. But I prayed for it secretly to Ganapati.'

'He certainly heard you,' said the grandfather, visibly moved.

'You'll tell us stories again, won't you?' said the father. 'I miss you already'.

'You have spoilt me, all of you,' said the guru. 'You know that I've been a monk for decades and that I spend my time between social work and study. But speaking of Shiva has made me feel more attached, not detached. Isn't that odd?'

'It's *Ishakripa* on us,' said the grandmother, her eyes moist.

'It's not odd at all,' said the grandfather. 'Like your beloved Acharya says, "*Matacha Parvati Devi, Pitadevo Maheshvaraha, Bandhava Shivabhaktascha, Svadesho Bhuvanatrayam*".'

'What does that mean?' said the child.

'My mother is Parvati, my father is Shiva, his worshippers are my friends and the three worlds are my country,' supplied the father.

'That is Acharya's way of saying that "everybody is my friend and everywhere I go is home",' said the guru to the child. 'That's how you're supposed to think if you sincerely salute Parvati and Shiva as the mother and father of the universe.'

'What about your room at the ashram? Will you be able to retain it while you're away? You have so many books,' said the grandfather.

'Not a problem. The Head Monk has been most kind. In fact, the ashram will even give me a small travel stipend since the Head Monk has some visits and discussions that he wants me to make on his behalf around the country,' said the guru.

'What about food and places to stay?' said the mother.

'The least of my problems,' said the guru. 'Almost any dharamshala, ashram or temple quarters will do. There are so many, all over India. Also, my ashram has branches and affiliations everywhere, more than even the State Bank of India, I should think.'

'What if you find yourself in a small, remote village?' said the grandmother.

'It's highly unlikely that the village panchayat will refuse me a meal or a place to sleep. I have restrictions about what I eat, not whose food I eat. I never had, even before I became a monk. And you know how hospitable our people are, in every community. What do I eat, anyway, as my daily fare? A piece of fruit, a glass of milk or chaas, a bit of khichri—or a roti and a small bowl of vegetables, that's more than plenty. The romance of the road and rail is alive even today if your needs are simple and you meet and greet people with respect. My only luxury will be a visit to local cyber cafés, where I find them, since my travel phone is very basic. I'll leave my smartphone behind for safety with the ashram office. Oh, and my other luxury will be a tube of Odomos, since no amount of meditation has made me immune to mosquitos,' laughed the guru.

'Indeed, I don't know how Acharya or anyone else stood it, or Rama, Sita and Lakshmana out in the jungle, back in the Dvapara Yuga. Perhaps there were no mosquitos then? As a boy, I always wondered about the point of having mosquitos and cockroaches as part of creation, until I read a wonderful story about the English scientist, J.B.S. Haldane. He became an Indian citizen, you know, and died in Bhubaneswar in 1964. When he was asked what we could conclude about the nature of the Creator from a study of creation, Haldane is said to have answered, "An inordinate fondness for beetles". It made me laugh so much that I developed a tolerance for most insects. That reminds me, I must pay my respects to Mahadev as Lingaraj at Bhubaneshwar.'

'Please keep in touch by email and call us now and then to let us know where you are,' said the grandfather.

'It sounds very exciting. I envy your freedom as a man and as a monk, to come and go as you please,' said the mother.

'I wish very much that our society would make it comfortable for women, too,' said the guru apologetically. 'It's had plenty of time to change and learn how to be decent and respectful. It's disgusting how badly some men behave. They harass and torture our women, and give our religion and culture a bad name. We cannot be proud of a culture if its living context is cruel or depraved.'

'That's one of the things I'm supposed to motivate various ashram heads and religious speakers to own and

operate. We want them to update their discourses to teach
society to be respectful of the rights and aspirations of all
women, not only married women with sons . . . respect
the rights and aspiration of every *person*, as our tradition
wants us to in theory. I had a long talk with the Head
Monk about our katha sessions and when I told him that
I yearned to go on a yatra because of the katha, he tasked
me with a mission. No Hindu can issue diktats since we
all own the religion. Shiva tells us so, Acharya tells us so.
But ashram heads and kathakars in the mother tongues
are persons of great influence across society. They could
do a lot to change the old mindset in a positive way. The
Head Monk thinks that a steady, one-to-one campaign of
persuasion to update our interpretations and nuance our
stories has a good chance. He wants to test the waters with
me as his emissary.'

'Good God! I had no idea that there were such wheels
within wheels,' said the grandfather. 'It's amazing to think
that our little family story sessions contain the seeds of
revolution. I wish your mission success and luck, Guruji.
Rather, I wish *us* luck—everyone in society, I mean.
I absolutely dread to think of the child growing up in a
hostile, predatory world.'

'I think it is well worth a try to talk *to* Hindus, not
at them like so many do,' said the grandmother, her eyes
kindling.

'I would really love to be able to freely travel around
like Teacher,' said the mother dreamily.

'And I would go with you, if we could both get away
from work,' said the father. 'We must plan a family holiday

to somewhere meaningful when Guruji is away. But where should we go first?'

'What do you say to Ujjain?' said the grandfather. 'It's not all that far and the Malwa Plateau is worth a look.'

'Revisit with the child, you mean, and refresh our own memories? That's a good idea.'

'I should love to go, I've never been there,' said the grandmother. 'How do we go, by train or plane?'

'There are flights from Delhi to Indore and then we have to go 50 km by road to Ujjain,' put in the mother, looking up from her phone.

'Good, we can begin to plan,' said the father.

'Guruji, let's have tea first, shall we?' said the grandmother. 'And after that, please will you tell us about Mahadev's lila at Ujjain? I would like to go there knowing that we have first visited it with you in spirit.'

'A most excellent plan,' said the guru. 'It is one of my favourite places for several reasons.'

The father excused himself to go to the study to scan the map, leaving the guru and the grandfather to chat. The mother and grandmother went away with the child to hurriedly put together a special tea as a small send-off to the guru. The grandmother had discovered some of his modest tastes over the years and it was with great affection that she made a fluffy poha with peanuts, peas and coconut, and crisp, hot, fried potato wedges to serve with coriander-mint chutney. Meanwhile, the child carefully arranged bowls of raisins and almonds as directed by her mother, who mixed apples, oranges, bananas, grapes and pomegranates into a fruit salad and poured thick, sweetened cream over it. The father and grandfather came to take the trays from them and over tea, which he thoroughly appreciated, the guru told them about some of the places he intended to visit.

After the tea things were cleared away, the family quietly arranged itself to face the guru. As he led them through the dear, familiar call and response, they felt a sharp pang to think that this would be their last story session for a long while. Afraid to cry, the child put out her hand to hold her mother's and the mother squeezed her hand, wanting very much to cry herself. The father, who sat between his parents, found himself holding a hand each and wished that he could cry, too. A great sense of loss gripped them all and they tried hard to blink back their tears.

The guru affected not to notice. Instead, he said, 'Before I begin to tell you about Mahadev's lila, will you join me in chanting the Ram Mantra that Parvati obtained for us from Shiva?'

The family managed to nod.

The guru led with *'Sri Rama Rama Rameti Rame Rame Manorame; Sahasranama Tattulyam Rama Nama Varanane*, the Ram Mantra from the Mahabharata in which Shiva told Parvati, "Beloved, just that one enchanting name Rama has the value of a thousand names."' The family repeated it after the guru and followed his cue to softly chant 'Rama, Rama, Rama, Rama, Rama . . .' instinctively closing their eyes. When the chanting was done and they looked up, they found that they felt restored and stable.

Satisfied that they had recovered emotionally, the guru began his story.

'Everyone knows of the importance of Kashi. But the story of Ujjain is even older. It takes us back to the very dawn of creation.'

'The oldest hymns say that out of nothing came nothing at all. Everything was complete already. So Creation was a whim of the gods, their lila. Their energies were unlimited and unending. Within them, they sensed life's longing for itself and let it happen. But with life was born the longing for liberation from it, in the hearts of many souls on earth. That is why Shiva, the Timeless Lord, came down from Mount Kailash to Ujjain. He wanted to stay with people and help them cross over to timelessness.'

'Ujjain was first called "Avantika" for it contained the *vana* or forests of healing herbs gifted to earth.'

'But then there came the ambitious asura, Tripur.'

'He performed the most terrible austerities and wrenched a boon from Brahma.'

'The boon was that he and his two brothers should have a floating city each in the sky, one made of gold, one of silver and one of iron. Nobody could destroy these cities except by one arrow when the three were in perfect alignment in the sky. Brahma was forced to grant his wish.'

'Secure in his supernatural power, Tripur unleashed great cruelty on the world. He took anything he fancied, tortured people and animals for sport, killed right and left, set fire to crops and forests for fun and dried up rivers and ponds, making daily life extremely dangerous and difficult for all three worlds, especially the earth. It was easier than he thought because the people on earth, particularly in rich, green Avantika, had become lazy and indifferent to the bounty of Nature around them. They failed to appreciate their blessings of sunshine, rain, rivers, trees, herbs and rich soil. Shiva and Parvati had given them everything, but instead of appreciating it, they were petty, quarrelsome and lacking in unity. They were easily invaded and destroyed by Tripur and his brothers.'

'Somehow, a few sincere and god-loving earthlings made their way to Mount Kailash in great secrecy and stealth, to fall at Lord Shiva's feet. "Save us from Tripur, Mahadev! We seek refuge in you," they begged piteously.'

'Shiva assured them that Tripur's end was close at hand.'

'Barely had they got back home when a strange, terrifying thing happened.'

'The sky took on an unnatural glow.'

'The earth became as a chariot drawn by war horses, with Brahma as the charioteer.'

'The sun and moon seemed to become its wheels.'

'The mighty Himalayas seemed to become a bow.'

'And on this bow, Lord Vishnu himself appeared as the arrow.'

'From this magical chariot, Lord Shiva rode across the sky and in that brief moment when the three cities were in alignment as they floated around the earth, he destroyed the three with that one arrow and with that, he destroyed Tripur. This feat was celebrated for evermore as "*Tripurardhan*", the "Destruction of Tripur".'

'Now, Tripur was less than a straw for Mahadev's might. Nevertheless, to refresh Creation with a sense of purpose, he had let this cosmic drama take place.'

'He bestowed on mankind a great sense of moral victory.'

'This outstanding victory or "*Uchhitam Vijay*" is remembered forever in the name "Ujjain".'

'There was peace for some time after that. But Ujjain's innate lustre, its rich land and ripe crops, made it a coveted prize for looters.'

'The next assault on this holy city was by an asura called Dushan.'

'However, when Shiva saw Dushan advancing as Kaal or Death on his devotees, he turned at once into Maha Kaal, the "Death of death". He destroyed Dushan with just one fiery breath.'

'"Maha Kaal" means both "the Death of death" and "Time". It is a richly layered word, also meaning "Eternity", "Immortality" and "Infinity".'

'The people of Ujjain begged Mahadev to stay in their midst always.'

'"Just knowing that you are here will give us courage forever to live and last through whatever may befall us," they prayed.'

'Shiva answered the prayers of his grateful devotees to abide forever in Ujjain as Mahakaleshwar, the Lord of Eternity.'

'He became a marvellous pillar of light, a Jyotirling, and the people of Ujjain fell to their knees in awe. The heavenly light faded, leaving behind a stone shivling. This represents Shiva as Mahakaleshwar in Ujjain even today.'

'There are twelve such Jyotirlings across India that mark the places where Shiva appeared in a crisis, blazed in glory as a pillar of light and left behind a symbol of himself.'

'Mahakaleshwar, as you know, is by the river Kshipra at Ujjain in Madhya Pradesh. It is the only svayambhu lingam or self-manifested marker of Shiva. The others were made holy by mantra shakti. They are:

Somnath by the western sea in Gujarat,
Mallikarjuna by the river Krishna at Srisailam in Andhra Pradesh,
Omkareshwar by the river Narmada, also in Madhya Pradesh,
Vaidyanath at Deogarh in the Santhal Parganas of Jharkhand,
Bhimashankar by the river Bhima in the Sahyadri hills near Pune in Maharashtra,
Rameshwaram at Ram Setu by the eastern sea in Tamil Nadu from where the bridge to Lanka was made to rescue Sita from Ravana,
Nageshwar, near the site of Dwaraka, Sri Krishna's city on the coast of Saurashtra in Gujarat,
Kashi Vishwanath, of course, by the Ganga in Uttar Pradesh,
Trimbakeshwar by the source of the river Godavari near Nashik in Maharashtra,
Kedarnath, 12,000 feet high on the mountain Kedar in the Rudra Himalaya range in Uttarakhand, which is one of the holiest sites in India,
and Grishneshwar at Ellora in Maharashtra.'

'The twelve Jyotirlingas hold up the sacred geography of India from Kedarnath in the high Himalayas to

Rameshwaram on the farthest coast of India. They have held us up emotionally from ancient times.'

'Of the twelve, the Mahakaleshwar Jyotirling is considered the centre point of earth from which time is reckoned. Ujjain was the Prime Meridian millennia before Greenwich. The ancient Romans knew it as "Ozene", a former royal capital, and imported "agate and carnelian, Indian muslins and mallow cloth" from Ujjain, "mallow" being an old word for jute. The Roman ships docked at "Barygaza" or Bharuch on the coast of Gujarat. We know this from *The Periplus of the Erythraean Sea*, an ancient Greco-Roman work from perhaps the mid-first century BCE.'

'In the old universe of discourse, it was said that a shivling in heaven and a shivling in the netherworld were in alignment with the Mahakaleshwar shivling, making Ujjain the *axis mundi* or "pillar of the earth" connecting the three worlds. That is why the central panchang or lunar calendar, which we still follow, is calculated even today from Ujjain. This is where we believe that Time began.'

'I had no idea that Ujjain was so very special,' said the mother.

'Yes, it has a unique and highly influential place in our lives even today, whether we know it or not. The shivling and the site are ancient but the structure of the temple has changed. We don't know what it may have looked like once. Iltutmish, the Sultan of Delhi, plundered the city and destroyed its temples in the thirteenth century, in 1235. But Ujjain remained important as a trade centre. Maharani Ahilyabai Holkar gave it a new lease of life in the eighteenth century. She was a brave, good queen who was widowed early but took charge when she had to, very competently and sincerely. She even led her troops until she acquired a military commander. She was the best Indian queen of all and one of the best rulers we ever had.'

'Ahilyabai died at the age of seventy. She ruled for a very supportive, productive thirty years as the queen of Malwa. Girls were not usually educated then but her father had taught her to read and write. She wanted everyone to come up, and supported all classes of society. She looked after the poor, gave her people good governance and did not use public funds for personal expenses. Can you imagine that, though she was queen? It was a golden age in the heart of India.'

'She became a legend in her lifetime, fiercely loved by her people and admired by other rulers, from the Nizam of Hyderabad to the British. Her capital was at the lovely town of Maheshwar by the Narmada. Poets, writers and artists flocked to her court. Using her personal funds, she rebuilt the Kashi Vishwanath temple and did a lot for many holy cities across India, including Ujjain—she built temples, wells, ghats, roads and rest houses. Later, in the nineteenth century, it was the British who decided to reduce the importance of Ujjain because its merchants were known to be anti-British. They made Indore important in its place, a fine town that had been developed from a sleepy little village by Maharani Ahilyabai.'

'I have a very nice "Maheshwari" handloom cotton sari,' confessed the grandmother. 'Ahilyabai invented the design and her present descendants revived it. I particularly like to wear it on 15 August in private celebration of Indian women.'

'Really, Ma? What a sweet thing to do. I must get one, too, though I don't wear saris as often as you,' said the mother. 'Ahilyabai sounds brilliant. I wish I had a good biography of her to read. How come we don't know enough about her in the normal course of things? When I was checking flights to Indore, I saw that the airport there is called Devi Ahilya Bai Holkar Airport. Now I know why.'

'I imagine Ujjain has a lot of temples, if it's so holy,' said the grandmother.

'The Panch Kos or pilgrim circuit of Ujjain takes us through eighty-four temples. It's an energy field like the Goverdhan Parikrama. Several temples in Ujjain were rebuilt on old, unforgotten sites during Ahilyabai's rule. But then, Ujjain remembers everything. When the stars are in alignment every twelve years over Ujjain for the great event of the Kumbh Mela, they say that the constellations in the sky are represented on earth by the city's temples.'

'Shakti is there, too, you know. The Harsiddhi Shaktipeeth at Ujjain is one of the fifty-one places where parts of Sati's body fell. This temple marks the site where Sati's elbow is believed to have fallen. The link with the goddess added the power of *siddhi* or enlightened understanding to Ujjain. It became known as a place of intellectual attainment.'

'That's why Sri Krishna was sent to study there with his brother Balarama at Rishi Sandipani's gurukul, where Sudama, too, was a student and became Krishna's friend.

Krishna was so adept that he learnt not only the warrior's skill of archery and the fourteen sciences but also "the sixty-four arts" from Guru Sandipani. Later, Krishna married Mitravinda, a princess of Ujjain. She was one of his eight chief queens.'

'Ujjain was also at the crossroads of important earthly political alliances between the ancient kingdoms of Magadha, Kosala, Vatsa and Avanti.'

'In the third century BCE, young prince Ashoka was sent by his father as the governor of Ujjain. Ashoka married Devi, a rich merchant's daughter from Vidisha, and his son, Prince Mahendra, was born in Ujjain. Ashoka went back to Pataliputra in Bihar but Queen Devi stayed on at Ujjain.'

'When Ashoka embraced Buddhism, it was from Ujjain that he sent his son Mahendra and daughter Sanghamitra to the eastern coast and out across the sea as missionaries to Sri Lanka. They were taught at Ujjain, which everyone knew of as a town of scholars.'

'It was at Ujjain, too, that King Bhartrihari once ruled. However, when disappointed in love, he became an ascetic and a recluse, living in a cave on the banks of the river Kshipra. He composed many profound verses that were widely spread by the Nath Sampradaya order of sadhus and are still sung in India. You must see "Bhartihari's Cave" by the Kshipra, when you visit.

'Then, in 57 BCE, King Vikramaditya of Ujjain won a famous victory over the Shakas. He founded a new era to commemorate this. Ahead of the Gregorian calendar by 57 years, the Vikram Era or Vikram Samvat is still in use with us as the Indian calendar.'

'Vikramaditya was a great and noble king who set a high standard of excellence. Many later kings tried to be like him and live up to his reputation.'

'Vikramaditya established a grand court at Ujjain. It attracted many great scholars and Ujjain further flourished in that period as a seat of learning.'

'Sciences like mathematics and astronomy, arts and literature achieved new heights during his rule. His court had the pick of eminent scientists and artistes. They were collectively known as the Navratna or Nine Gems, a concept picked up by later rulers.'

'Among them was the great physician and healer Dhanvantari, a master of Ayurveda and the author of an important medical treatise.'

'Varahamihira was a well-known astronomer and astrologer whose fame spread to faraway kingdoms as did the news of his specially built observatory at Ujjain. It disappeared under the debris of history but was never forgotten. Centuries later, Maharaja Jai Singh II of Jaipur managed to build an observatory there as an act of reparation.'

'Vetal Bhat, author of the still-popular *Vetal Pacheesi* or *Twenty-five Tales of the Ghoul*, wrote elegant, witty stories that not only entertained but also served as lessons in character-building, ethics, best practices and diplomacy for kings and commoners alike.'

'Vararuchi, the great grammarian, wrote a formidable work on Prakrit grammar. He is also said to have authored the collection of stories called *Simhasan Batteesi* or *Thirty-two Tales of the Throne*.'

'I know those stories,' said the child. 'Papa and I read them together. I like Vikram and Vetal—and Raja Bhoj of Malwa in the *Throne* stories'.

'You're not scared of the Vetal?'

'Papa says I don't have to be because the Vetal can never get past King Vikram.'

'Anyway, what's a Vetal compared to the Shivaganas, eh?'

'They don't scare me either. They can't help looking different. Ma says if they're good enough for Mahadev, they're good enough for us.'

'And quite right, too. Those stories from Ujjain are still with us, and also the poems and plays of Kalidasa whose *Kumarasambhavam* you know about. He was from Ujjain, too. In fact, several famous ancient plays are set in Ujjain by other playwrights like Bhasa and Shudraka.'

'We consider Kalidasa the finest Sanskrit playwright and poet. We don't really know his history but his works remain a reality. Well, you've seen how the known and the Unknown seamlessly interface throughout the land via its sacred geography. The depth and range of the concept are unique to India. Think of Ratnavati and the rock-solid Thayumanavar temple at Trichy or Nakkeeran at Madurai who left behind an actual literary work on Kumar, or Ram Setu or Mathura–Vrindavan or Kashi or a thousand other places.'

'So I can't resist telling you a popular tale about Kalidasa. Parvati was the turning point in his story and he repaid his debt to her magnificently with *Kumarasambhavam*. She helped him save his marriage and he retold the story of her wedding with divine inspiration, in divine language. The legend of Kalidasa is the true stuff of literary romance.'

'We don't know his original name but the story goes that he was an illiterate local youth who was picked up and married through a palace intrigue to the learned princess Vidyottama of Ujjain.'

'After the wedding, the princess was terribly shocked to discover her husband's complete lack of learning. He couldn't even write his own name. The princess, who worshipped Shiva and Parvati with total faith, now prayed desperately to them to save her from this shame and misery. Swallowing her anger at the way she had been tricked by cunning ministers at court who resented her learning and feared that she might even be queen one day, she told the country bumpkin to pray to Parvati to help him get an education.'

'He went weeping to a temple nearby where Parvati was worshipped as Ma Kali and spoke to her with such honesty and in such a childlike, funny way that she found him amusing. She took pity on him, and on the poor princess whose dignity was now so shatteringly at stake, and blessed him with instant wit, learning and poetic skill. His mind suddenly lit up with wise, beautiful thoughts, with words and rhymes and meters and metaphors. Encouraged by Parvati, he went back bravely to the princess and told her that the goddess had blessed him and that he wished to be called "Kalidasa", the devotee of Ma Kali.'

'To test him, the princess asked him a question in Sanskrit: "*Asti kashchit vaagvisheshah*?" "Is there something unique to speech?" meaning, "Have you anything special to say?"'

'Kalidasa smiled sunnily and told her to give him some time to answer. He went to live by the Kali temple and wrote steadily every day between prayers to the divine mother. He began three enormous poems with those very words, as a grand answer that there *is* something to speech.'

'His epic poem *Kumarasambhavam* about the marriage of Shiva and Parvati begins with the word "*Asti*".'

'The epic poem *Raghuvamsha* or "Lineage of Sri Rama" begins with the word "*Vaak*".'

'"*Kashchit*" occurs in the first stanza of *Meghdoot*, "The Cloud-Messenger"—the lyric poem that vividly describes the beauty of the north Indian landscape with Ujjain as the jewel in its crown dedicated to Mahakaleshwar.'

'And we can't possibly forget his most famous play, *Abhignyana-Shaakuntalam,* "The Recognition of Shakuntala".'

'What a romantic story. He arrived illiterate and came back a great poet. Did Vidyottama and Kalidasa live happily ever after?' said the grandmother.

'I think it's safe to say that they must have. What a story . . . *asti kashchit vaagvisheshah*. Maybe it was that which inspired Kalidasa to describe Shiva and Parvati as "*vaak*" and "*arth*", inseparable as "word" and "meaning". He wrote three plays and four long epic poems in Sanskrit.'

'I heard from a friend just last week that the Shillong Youth Choir was going to sing Schubert's unfinished opera *Shakuntala* at the Austrian Embassy,' said the mother.

'Shakuntala went west in a big way in the colonial period,' said the grandfather.

'I wish I knew something by Kalidasa,' said the mother. 'They taught me *Lord Ullin's Daughter* and *The Inchcape Rock* in school, and sonnets by Shakespeare. Not that I mind knowing those poems. English poetry is quite charming. But it would have been nice to have learnt something by Kalidasa to balance east and west. Beyond our Hindi textbooks, I mean. I can't help feeling that I belong to a cheated generation.'

'You would probably have learnt about *asti kashchit vaagvisheshah* in the eighth standard if your school had taught you Sanskrit. Mine did not either, it was very, very Westernized, which is useful out in the world but leaves you trapped in the English language with a big, empty hole in your heart. So I struggled to learn Sanskrit privately. My first textbook was the *Laghu Siddhanta Kaumudi*. It's an abridged version of Panini's Sanskrit grammar by someone called Varadaraja back in the seventeenth century. I almost gave up! But luckily I found a very sweet old teacher with a genuine love of the language, a sanyasi at the Kanchi Kamakshi temple opposite the Jawaharlal Nehru University East Gate. My ashram helped me a lot, too. And once it takes hold, you never want to stop.'

'However, you can still obtain a real piece of Kalidasa through other, informal ways. I'd like to give you some nice homework while I'm away, which I'll take you through when I come back. Will you look up Kalidasa's prayer to Parvati as the giver of wisdom? It's supposed to be his very first composition, a paean of thanks after she blessed him with instant scholarship. It's very beautiful and powerful . . . "*sarva tantratmike sarva yantratmike* (need English here)". You can find it on YouTube. It's called *Sri Shyamala Dandakam,* and begins with the words "*Manikya veenam upalayalantim*" (the soul of all magic and occult power). There are several versions out there, some very long, but I have a soft spot for the one chanted by Bharat Ratna M.S. Subbulakshmi. It's about seven minutes long. Her pronunciation is perfect and her *bhakti bhava* is sublime.'

'I shall find it and we shall learn it,' said the mother resolutely. 'I would love to recite something by Kalidasa on the banks of the Kshipra. If I don't manage to learn it by heart before our trip, I'll hear it on YouTube by the river.'

'We'll all hear it. Imagine hearing Kalidasa in Ujjain. But why is the Kumbh Mela celebrated there?' said the father.

'Ah, for that, we must go right back to the story of the Kalakuta poison which Shiva drank to save the world.'

'When amrita, the nectar or elixir of eternal life, emerged in a jar from the Ocean of Milk, a drop each fell on Ujjain, Prayag, Nashik and Haridwar, making them sacred sites.'

'Our chance to obtain an earthly share of the elixir comes once in twelve years at each of those four places, when the stars are in the very same alignment as they were above each city when the drop of nectar fell on it. This event is called the Kumbh or Jar after the jar of amrita. They call it Singhast in Ujjain because Guru or Jupiter is in Simha or Leo then over the city.'

'If you go to Ujjain during the month-long Singhast, the tradition of countless pilgrims is to follow the Panch Kos pilgrim circuit, have a cleansing dip in the Kshipra and then go to Mahakaleshwar in spiritual surrender.'

'We've missed the 2016 Singhast, which means there won't be another until 2028,' mourned the grandmother.

'I'm told that 75 million people showed up during the month of the 2016 Singhast. There was no proper Kumbh Mela at Ujjain for centuries, you know. The present Singhast Kumbh was revived in the eighteenth century by the Maratha ruler Ranoji Shinde who patterned it after the Nashik Kumbh, which itself is patterned on the Haridwar Kumbh. In fact, the Ujjain Singhast is the only Kumbh to have been revived in a princely state. The others took place in British-ruled cities.'

'Then, there's the south Indian Kumbh at the ancient temple town of Kumbakonam by the Kaveri, in Tamil Nadu. Kumbakonam was a big centre of Hindu culture and European education. It was called "the Cambridge of south India" during the colonial period. The Kumbh there is called "Mahamaham". It's held every twelve years for ten days when Jupiter is in Leo. The brightest star in Leo is Regulus, known to us as Magha nakshatra. Hence the name "Maha Magham" that softened over time to "Mahamaham".'

'Many sacred rivers of India are believed to turn up in the Kumbakonam tank during that time—Ganga, Yamuna, Godavari, Narmada, Mahanadi, Sarayu, Sindhu, Kaveri, Payoshini—the Mahabharata's name for the Tapti . . . and even the hidden Sarasvati.'

'That's incredible,' said the grandfather. 'It reminds me of something my father once told me about how one did a full Kashi Yatra. He said we had to take a pot of water from the Ganga to pour into the sea at Ram Setu and vice versa.'

'Yes, it's *Aa Setu Himalaya* in reverse currents of affirmation. I'm told that Mansar Lake in Jammu, by which there is an Umapati-Mahadev temple, is where the devout take a dip on holy days. Mansar represents Mansarovar in Jammu. There are layers of connection across India that will take the westernized minority like us years to fully discover. If you remember, I noticed it in Himachal Pradesh, too, at Paragpur. I'm sure Acharya noticed it long before any of us.'

'It's a tight, wide web that was deeply embedded in the land millennia ago, that remains deeply embedded in innumerable heads, even ours. People like us may appear to merely skim the surface but it goes deep with us, too. See how hungrily we respond to our prayers and stories, our tirthas and kshetras, and to anything good and beautiful in our tradition. Wherever we are, we feel the thrilling connection with the gods who make our geography sacred. Mirabai said it for us, "*Chalo mann, Ganga-Jamuna teer*— oh heart let us go to Ganga-Yamuna".

'That's why lakhs of people arrive at Kumbakonam for a mass-bathing ceremony with no issues about who belongs to which community. Every class and caste shows up and cheerfully bathes together, women, too. Taking Shiva-Parvati's name, and Vishnu's, they dissolve their identities in the waters and pray to emerge with their heart and karma cleansed. Luckily, the tank is big. It covers 6.2 acres and is shaped like a trapezoid.'

'The whole town pitches in for those ten days for Annadanam, the giving of food. That is our most important religious duty, you know, more than any ceremony. You may never go to a temple but if you feed the poor, the travellers and the pilgrims, you can chalk up some very good karma. Every temple and ashram cooks for the crowd and so do private households. The Muslims of Kumbakonam contribute a thousand kilos of rice each time towards the Mahamaham Annadanam. Anybody can show up anywhere for a meal. It's all quite wonderful.'

'That's so heartwarming to know,' said the grandmother. 'To think that Shiva drank poison to save the world so long ago and we still thank him on such a scale, up and down the land. Kumbh is a beautiful, inclusive idea. It should bring out the best in people.'

'All year round and every year, not just every twelve years,' snorted the grandfather.

'Our fasts, feasts and festivals are daily reminders and Kumbh is a big, collective reminder,' said the guru gently.

'What should we do when we go to Ujjain?' said the father.

'You could go to the early morning bhasma *harati* of Mahakaleshwar at 4 a.m. that only men used to go to because of the early hour. But any one of us can book it online today and watch it being conducted. It's free. You need to book only because the space is limited inside, so they issue passes for which you need ID proof. Or you could just go to the large temple hall and watch it onscreen.

Ladies have to wear saris and men have to wear dhotis if they want to attend the ash *harati*.'

'They do the ablution or jal abhishek before the bhasma *harati*. *Abhishekha priyo Shiva*, remember? The jal abhishek is from 3.15 a.m. to 4 a.m. I'm told that you have to be in line by about one in the morning because it's "first come, first in line".'

'What if you're not a morning person?' said the mother.

'Mahadev doesn't mind at all. You can go any time when the temple is open. They are quite relaxed about the dress code otherwise. Any day is good for Mahakaleshwar. There is an endless cycle of puja and *harati* Monday prayers, prayers for the day, for the week, for the month, for the year. Every temple in Ujjain has its own cycle. Ujjain had a cosy, happy atmosphere with its calendar of festivals and feasts. I felt that I was part of a living tradition.'

'I do wish you would come with us,' said the grandfather.

'Please come, Teacher,' said the child.

The guru looked at them fondly. He liked them very much and had every intention of coming back to Delhi to tell them more stories and teach the child to read and write the language of the gods. He looked forward to sharing his own love of prose and poetry. Many pleasant days lay assuredly ahead, delightful times of song and story.

But now, it was time to go and wander alone around the land he loved. 'Shivbhumi,' he thought and chuckled silently, thinking of cake. That would have amused and pleased Mahadev and Parvati.

He felt a rush of glad warmth in his heart. 'They're laughing inside me,' he thought and got up to leave.

'Let me know when you plan to visit Ujjain,' he said. 'Perhaps we'll meet by the Kshipra and if we're lucky, we'll get to see Mahadev together, at least a glimpse, like Narada at Bhadragiri. "*Mahimna paaram te parama vidusho yadya sadrushi*—Even very wise people have not seen the far shore of your greatness", as Pushpadanta said to Shiva once upon a time.'